LAST DAYS OF THE DOG-MEN

"Vibrant, hopeful, even in the face of certain heartbreak . . . It's this vision, this intelligent and evocative quest for understanding, that truly marks Brad Watson's stories."

—*New York Newsday*

"Watson's stories do not so much end as they resonate, and this resonance keeps the reader wondering, probing, thinking, and ultimately reading on." —*Bookpage*

"With tender sympathy, no sentimentality and an almost preternatural insight into the antithetical souls of these complementary species, the stories in *Last Days of the Dog-Men* are weird and wise, sometimes gruesome and often brilliant."

—*The New York Times Book Review*

"TERRIFIC! BRAD WATSON CAN WRITE."

—*Chattanooga Times* (Tenn.)

"A POWERFUL DEBUT BY A MASTER STORYTELLER . . . BRAD WATSON'S STORIES ARE WHOLLY ORIGINAL—HUMOROUS AND HEARTBREAKING."

—Jill McCorkle

"Brad Watson is a writer still mystified by his own immense talent. How could he not be? He writes sentences you wait a lifetime for. Tells stories you've never heard. *Last Days of the Dog-Men* is the best I've read in ages. Mercy for none, but salvation for all." —Robert Olmstead

Please turn the page for more extraordinary acclaim. . . .

"COMPELLING!" —*Elle*

"POWERFUL . . . Watson's muscular prose stands shoulder to shoulder with the best cracker realists, from Faulkner to Larry Brown." —*Kirkus Reviews*

"Watson has uncanny insight into canine psychology and, beyond that, into how people project their own emotions, aggression, love and insecurities onto pets and the animal kingdom." —*Publishers Weekly*

"HERE ARE STORIES WRITTEN IN BRACING PROSE, HERALDING THE ARRIVAL OF A NEW TALENT ON THE LITERARY SCENE." —*Tuscaloosa News* (Ala.)

"THE PROSE IS CRISP . . . RIFE WITH SPIRITED GOOD HUMOR AND HIGH INTELLIGENCE."
—Pinckney Benedict

"Brad Watson's prose is exciting, superb. Not a dull story here. Dogs? Well, often they're more interesting than their masters, certainly more abiding. Watson's people are the wretched dreams of honorable dogs. I read these pieces with great pleasure." —Barry Hannah

LAST DAYS OF THE DOG-MEN

Stories

Brad Watson

A Delta Book
Published by
Dell Publishing
a division of
Bantam Doubleday Dell Publishing Group, Inc.
1540 Broadway
New York, New York 10036

"The Wake" was originally published in *Dog Stories*, edited by Kevin R. Kaszubowski.
"Seeing Eye" and "Bill" were originally published in *Story Magazine*.
"Kindred Spirits" first appeared in slightly different form in the *Oxford American*.

The text of this book is composed in Linotype Walbaum with the display set in Cloister Open.

ISBN: 0-385-31827-8

Reprinted by arrangement with W.W. Norton & Company, Inc.

Manufactured in the United States of America
Published simultaneously in Canada

August 1997

10 9 8 7 6 5 4 3 2 1
BVG

For Jason, Owen, Bonnie,
and Jeanine

CONTENTS

Thanks to Jon Hershey, Ric Dice, Stephanie Bobo, and Will Blythe, gentle critics and friends; to the Horns for October writing quarters; to Lois Rosenthal for support and assistance; and to my brother Craig and my late father, Robert Earl Watson, great storytellers. Special thanks to Alane Salierno Mason, friend and editor, who made all the difference.

Ultimately, the dog, . . . its constant presence in human experience coupled with its nearness to the feral world, is the alter ego of man himself.

—David Gordon White,
Myths of the Dog-Man

LAST DAYS OF THE DOG-MEN

WHEN I WAS A BOY MY FAMILY ALWAYS HAD HUNTing dogs, always bird dogs, once a couple of blueticks, and for six years anywhere from six to fifteen beagles. But we never really got to where we liked to eat rabbit, and we tired of the club politics of hunting deer, so we penned up the beagles, added two black Labs, and figured we'd do a little duck.

Those were raucous days around the house, the big pen in the back with the beagles squawling, up on their hind legs against the fence, making noises like someone was cutting their tails off. It was their way. At night when I crept out into the yard they fell silent, their white necks exposed to the moon, their soft round eyes upon me. They made small, disturbed, guttural sounds like chickens.

Neighbors finally sent the old man to municipal court charged with something like disturbing the peace, and since my mother swore that anyway she'd never fry another rabbit, they looked like little bloody babies once skinned, she said, he farmed out the beagles and spent his Saturdays visiting this dog or that, out to Uncle Spurgeon's to see Jimbo, the best runner of the pack. Or out to Bud's rambling shack, where Bud lived with old Patsy and Balls, the breeder. They hollered like nuclear warning sirens when the old man drove up in his Ford.

After that he went into decline. He liked the Labs but never took much interest, they being already a hollow race of dog, the official dog of the middle class. He let them lounge around the porch under the ceiling fan and lope around the yard and the neighborhood, aimless loafers, and took to watching war movies on TV in his room, wandering through the house speaking to us like we were neighbors to hail, engage in small talk, and bid farewell. He was a man who had literally abandoned the hunt. He was of the generation that had moved to the city. He was no longer a man who lived among dogs.

It wasn't long after that I moved out anyway, and got married to live with Lois in a dogless suburban house, a quiet world that seemed unanchored somehow, half inhabited, pale and blank, as if it would one day dissolve to fog, lines blurring, and seep away into air, as indeed it would. We bought a telescope and spent some nights in the yard tracking the cold lights of the stars and planets, looking for patterns, never suspecting that here were the awful bloody secrets of the ancient human heart and that every generation must flesh them out anew. Humans are aware of very little, it seems to me, the artificial brainy side of life, the worries and bills and the mechanisms of jobs, the doltish psychologies we've placed over our lives like a stencil. A dog keeps his life simple and unadorned. He is who he is, and his only task is to assert this. If he desires the company of another dog, or if he wishes to mate, things can get a little complex. But the ways of settling such things are established and do not change. And when they are settled and he is home from his wandering he may have a flickering moment, a sort of Pickett's Charge across the synaptic field toward reflection. But the moment passes. And when it passes it leaves him with a vague disquietude, a clear nose that on a good night could smell the lingering presence of men on the moon, and the rest of the day ahead of him like a canyon.

WHICH IS HOW I'VE TRIED TO VIEW THE DAYS I'VE spent here in this old farmhouse where I'm staying with my friend Harold in the country. I'm on extended leave of absence from the *Journal.* But it's no good. It's impossible to bring that sort of order and clarity to a normal human life.

The farmhouse is a wreck floating on the edge of a big untended pasture where the only activities are the occasional squadron of flaring birds dropping from sight into the tall grass, and the creation of random geometric paths the nose-down dogs make tracking the birds. The back porch has a grand view of the field, and when weather permits we sit on the porch and smoke cigarettes and sip coffee in the mornings, beer in the afternoons, often good scotch at night. At midday, there's horseshoes.

There's also Phelan Holt, a mastiff of a man, whom Harold met at the Blind Horse Bar and Grill and allowed to rent a room in the house's far corner. We don't see a great deal of Phelan, who came down here from Ohio to teach poetry at the women's college. He once played linebacker for a small college in the Midwest, and then took his violent imagination to the page and published a book of poems about the big subjects: God, creation, the confusion of the animals, and the bloody concoction of love. He pads along a shiny path he's made through the dust to the kitchen for food and drink, and then pads back, and occasionally comes out to the porch to drink bourbon and to give us brief, elliptical lectures on the likes of Isaac Babel, Rilke, and Cervantes, gently smoking a joint which he does not share. In spite of his erudition, thick, balding Phelan is very much a moody old dog. He lives alone with others, leaves to conduct his business, speaks very little, eats moderately, and is generally inscrutable.

One day Harold proposed to spend the afternoon fishing for bream. We got into the truck and drove through a couple of pastures and down an old logging road through a patch of woods to a narrow cove that spread out into the broad sunlit surface of a lake. The sun played on thin rippling lines that spread from the small heads of snapping turtles and water moccasins moving now and then like sticks in a current.

Harold pulled a johnboat from the willows and rowed us out. We fished the middle, dropping our baits over what Harold said was the old streambed where a current of cooler water ran through down deep. The water was a dark coppery stain, like thin coffee. We began to pull up a few bluegill and crappie, and Phelan watched them burst from the water, broad flat gold and silver, and curl at the end of the line, their eyes huge. They flopped crazily in the bottom of the boat, drowning in the thin air. Phelan set down his pole and nipped at a half-pint of bourbon he'd pulled from his pocket.

"Kill it," he said, looking away from my bluegill. "I can't stand to watch it struggling for air." His eyes followed the tiny heads of moccasins moving silently across the surface, turtles lumbering onto half-submerged logs. "Those things will eat your fish right off the stringer," he said. He drank from the little bottle again and then in his best old-fashioned pedagogical manner said, "Do we merely project the presence of evil upon God's creatures, in which case we are inherently evil and the story of the garden a ruse, or is evil absolute?"

From his knapsack he produced a pistol, a Browning .22 semiautomatic that looked like a German Luger, and set it on his lap. He pulled out a sandwich and ate it slowly. Then he shucked a round into the gun's chamber and sighted down on one of the turtles and fired, the sharp report flashing off the water into the trees. What looked like a puff of smoke spiffed from the turtle's back and it tumbled from the log. "It's off a little to the right," he said. He aimed at a moccasin head crossing at the opposite bank and fired. The water jumped in front of the snake, which stopped, and Phelan quickly tore up the water where the head was with three quick shots. The snake disappeared. Silence, in the wake of the loud hard crack of the pistol, came back to our ears in shock waves over the water. "Hard to tell if you've hit them when they're swimming," he said, looking down the length of the barrel as if for flaws, lifting his hooded eyes to survey the water's surface for more prey.

HAROLD HIMSELF IS SORT OF LIKE A GARMENT DRAWN from the irregular bin: off-center, unique, a little tilted on his axis. If he were a dog, I'd call him an unbrushed collie who carries himself like a chocolate Lab. He has two actual dogs, a big blond hound named Otis and a bird dog named Ike. Like Phelan, Otis is a socialized dog and gets to come into the house to sleep, whereas Ike must stay outside on the porch. At first I could not understand why Otis received this privilege and Ike did not, but in time I began to see.

Every evening after supper when he is home, Harold gets up from the table and lets in Otis, who sits beside the table and looks at Harold, watching Harold's hands. Harold's hands pinching off a last bite of cornbread and nibbling on it, Harold's hands pulling a Camel cigarette out of the pack, Harold's hands twiddling with the matches. And soon, as if he isn't really thinking of it, in the middle of talking about something else and not even seeming to plan to do it, Harold will pick up a piece of meat scrap and let it hover over the plate for a minute, talking, and you'll see Otis get alert and begin to quiver almost unnoticeably. And then Harold will look at Otis and maybe say, "Otis, stay." And Otis's eyes will cut just for a second to Harold's and then snatch back to the meat scrap, maybe having to chomp his jaws together to suck saliva, his eyes glued to the meat scrap. And then Harold will gently lower the meat scrap onto the top of Otis's nose and then slowly take away his hand, saying, "Stay. Stay. Stay. Otis. Stay." Crooning it real softly. And Otis with his eyes cross-eyed looking at the meat scrap on his nose, quivering almost unnoticeably and not daring to move, and then Harold leans back and takes another Camel out of the pack, and if Otis slowly moves just an eighth of an inch, saying, "Otis. Stay." And then lighting the cigarette and then looking at Otis for a second and then saying, "All right, Otis." And quicker than you can see it Otis has not so much tossed the scrap up in the air as he has removed his nose from its position, the meat scrap suspended, and before it can begin to respond to gravity Otis has snatched it into his mouth and swallowed it and is looking at Harold's hands again with the same look as if nothing has happened between them at all and he is hoping for his first scrap.

This is the test, Harold says. If you balance the meat scrap, and in a moment of grace manage to eat the meat scrap, you are in. If you drop the meat scrap and eat it off of the floor, well, you're no better than a dog. Out you go.

But the thing I was going to tell at first is about Ike, about how when Otis gets let in and Ike doesn't, Ike starts barking outside the door, big woofing barks, loud complaints, thinking (Harold says), Why is he letting in Otis and not me? Let me IN. IN. And he continues his barking for some couple of minutes or so, and then, without your really being able to put your finger on just how it happens, the bark begins to change, not so much a complaint as a demand, I am IKE, let me IN, because what is lost you see is the memory of Otis having been let in first and that being the reason for complaint. And from there he goes to his more common generic statement, voiced simply because Ike is Ike and needs no reason for saying it, I am IKE, and then it changes in a more noticeable way, just IKE, as he loses contact with his ego, soon just Ike!, tapering off, and in a minute it's just a bark every now and then, just a normal call into the void the way dogs do, yelling HEY every now and then and seeing if anyone responds across the pasture, HEY, and then you hear Ike circle and drop himself onto the porch floorboards just outside the kitchen door. And this, Harold says, is a product of Ike's consciousness, that before he can even finish barking Ike has forgotten what he's barking about, so he just lies down and goes to sleep. And this, Harold says, as if the meat scrap test needs corroboration, is why Ike can't sleep indoors and Otis can.

THE OTHER DAY, HAROLD SAT IN A CHAIR IN FRONT OF HIS bedroom window, leaned back, and put his feet on the sill, and the whole window, frame and all, fell out into the weeds with a crash. I helped him seal the hole with polyethylene sheeting and duct tape and now there's a filtered effect to the light in the room that's quite nice on cool late afternoons.

There are clothes in the closets here, we don't know who they belong to. The front room and the dark attic are crammed with junk. Old space heaters in a pile in one corner, a big wooden canoe (cracked) with paddles, a set of barbells made from truck axles and wheel rims, a seamstress dummy with nipples painted on the breasts, some great old cane fly rods not too limber anymore, a big wooden Motorola radio, a rope ladder, a box of *Life* magazines, and a big stack of yellow newspapers from Mobile. And lots of other junk too numerous to name.

All four corners of the house slant toward the center, the back of the foyer being the floor's lowest point. You put a golf ball on the floor at any point in the house and it'll roll its way eventually, bumping lazily into baseboards and doors and discarded shoes and maybe a baseball mitt or a rolled-up rug slumped against the wall, to that low spot in the tall empty foyer where there's a power-line spool heaped with wadded old clothes like someone getting ready for a yard sale cleaned out some dresser drawers and disappeared. The doors all misfit their frames, and on gusty mornings I have awakened to the dry tick and skid of dead leaves rolling under the gap at the bottom of the front door and into the foyer, rolling through the rooms like little tumbleweeds, to collect in the kitchen, where then in ones and twos and little groups they skitter out the open door to the backyard and on out across the field. It's a pleasant way to wake up, really. Sometimes I hang my head over the side of the big bed I use, the one with four rough-barked cedar logs for posts and which Harold said the mice used before I moved in, and I'll see this big old skink with pink spots on his slick black hide hunting along the crevice between the baseboard and the floor. His head disappears into the crevice, and he draws it out again chewing something, his long lipless jaws chomping down.

The house doors haven't seen a working lock in thirty or forty years. Harold never really thinks about security, though the bums walking on the road to Florida pass by here all the time and probably used this as a motel before Harold found it out here abandoned on his family's land and became an expatriate from town because, he says, he never again wants to live anywhere he can't step out onto the back porch and take a piss day or night.

The night I showed up looking for shelter I just opened up the front door because no one answered and I didn't know if Harold was way in the back of the big old house (he was) or what. I entered the foyer, and first I heard a clicking sound and Otis came around the corner on his toes, claws tapping, his tail high, with a low growl. And then Harold eased in behind him, his rusty old .38 in his hand. He sleeps with it on a bookshelf not far from his bed, the one cheap bullet he owns next to the gun if it hasn't rolled off onto the floor.

The night that Phelan arrived to stay, fell through the door onto his back, and lay there looking up into the shadows of the high old foyer, Otis came clicking in and approached him slowly, hackles raised, lips curling fluidly against his old teeth, until his nose was just over Phelan's. And then he jumped back barking savagely when Phelan burst out like some slurring old thespian, "There plucking at his throat a great black beast shaped like a hound, 'The Hound!,' cried Holmes, 'Great Heavens!' half animal half demon, its eyes aglow its muzzles and hackles and dewlap outlined in flickering flame."

"Phelan," Harold said, "meet Otis."

"Cerberus, you mean," Phelan said, "my twelfth labor." He raised his arms and spread his fingers before his eyes. "I have only my hands."

How Harold came to be alone is this: Sophia, a surveyor for the highway department, fixed her sights on Harold and took advantage of his ways by drinking with him till two a.m. and then offering to drive him home, where she would put him to bed and ride him like a cowgirl. She told me this herself one night, and asked me to feel of her thighs, which were hard and bulging as an ice skater's under her jeans. "I'm strong," she whispered in my ear, cocking an eyebrow.

One evening, after she'd left, Harold stumbled out onto the porch where I sat smoking, bummed a cigarette, braced an arm against a porch post, and stood there taking a long piss out into the yard. He didn't say anything. He was naked. His hair was like a sheaf of windblown wheat against the moonlight coming down on the field and cutting a clean line of light along the edge of the porch. His pale body blue in that light. He kept standing there, his stream arcing out into the yard, sprayed to the east in the wind, breathing through his nose and smoking the cigarette with the smoke whipping away. There was a storm trying to blow in. I didn't have to say anything. You always know when you're close to out of control.

Sophia left paraphernalia around for Harold's fiancée Westley to find. Pairs of panties under the bed, a silky camisole slumped like a prostitute between two starched dress shirts in Harold's closet, a vial of fingernail polish in the silverware tray. It wasn't long before Westley walked out of the bathroom one day with a black brassiere, saying, "What's this thing doing hanging on the commode handle?" And it was pretty much over between Westley and Harold after that.

I must say that Sophia, who resembled a greyhound with her long nose and close-set eyes and her tremendous thighs, is the bridge between Harold's story and mine.

Because at first I wasn't cheating on Lois. Things

had become distant in the way they do after a marriage struggles through passionate possessive love and into the heartbreak of languishing love, before the vague incestuous love of the long-together. I got home one night when Lois and I were still together, heard something scramble on the living-room floor, and looked over to see this trembling thing shaped like a drawn bow, long needle-nose face looking at me as if over reading glasses, nose down, eyes up, cowed. He was aging. I eased over to him and pulled back ever so softly when as I reached my hand over he showed just a speck of white tooth along his black lip.

"I read that story in the *Journal* about them, and what happens to them when they can't race anymore," she said. She'd simply called up the dog track, gone out to a kennel, and taken her pick.

She said since he was getting old, maybe he wouldn't be hard to control, and besides, she thought maybe I missed having a dog. It was an attempt, I guess, to make a connection. Or it was the administration of an opiate. I don't really know.

To exercise Spike, the retired greyhound, and to encourage a friendship between him and me, Lois had the two of us, man and dog, take up jogging. We'd go to the high school track, and Spike loved it. He'd trot about on the football field, snuffling here and there. Once he surprised and caught a real rabbit, and tore it to pieces. It must have brought back memories of his training days. You wouldn't think a racing dog could be like a pet dog, foolish and simple and friendly. But Spike was okay. We were pals. And then, after all the weeks it took Spike and me to get back into shape, and after the incidental way in which my affair with Imelda down the street began out of our meeting and jogging together around the otherwise empty track, after weeks of capping our jog with a romp on the foam-rubber pole vault mattress just beyond the goalposts, Lois bicycled down to get me one night and rode silently up as Imelda and I lay naked except for our jogging shoes on the pole vault mattress, cooling down, Spike curled up at our feet. As she glided to a stop on the bicycle, Spike raised his head and wagged his tail. Seeing his true innocence, I felt a heavy knot form in my chest. When Lois just as silently turned the bicycle and pedaled away, Spike rose, stretched, and followed her home. Imelda and I hadn't moved.

"Oh, shit," Imelda said. "Well, I guess it's all over."

Imelda merely meant our affair, since her husband was a Navy dentist on a cruise in the Mediterranean, which had put Imelda temporarily in her parents' hometown, temporarily writing features for the *Journal*, and temporarily having an affair with me. It was Imelda's story on greyhounds that Lois had seen. It was Imelda who said she wanted to meet Spike, and it was I who knew exactly how this would go and gave in to the inexorable flow of it, combining our passive wills toward this very moment. And it was I who had to go home to Lois now that my marriage was ruined.

IMELDA LEFT, AND I LAY THERE AWHILE LOOKING UP AT the stars. It was early October, and straight up I could see the bright clusters of Perseus, Cassiopeia, Cepheus, Cygnus, and off to the right broad Hercules, in his flexing stance. I remembered how Lois and I used to make up constellations: there's my boss, she'd say, scratching his balls. There's Reagan's brain, she'd say. Where? The dim one. Where? That was the joke. Looking up at night usually made me feel as big as the sky, but now I felt like I was floating among them and lost. I got up and started the walk home. There was a little chill in the air, and the drying sweat tightened my skin. I smelled Imelda on my hands and wafting up from my shorts.

The door was unlocked. The lamp was on in the corner of the living room. The night-light was on in the hallway. I took off my running shoes and walked quietly down the hallway to the bedroom. I could see in the dim light that Lois was in bed, either asleep or pretending to be, facing the wall, her back to the doorway, the covers pulled up to her ears. She was still.

From my side of the bed, Spike watched me sleepily, stretched out, his head resting on his paws. I don't imagine I'd have had the courage to climb into bed and beg forgiveness, anyway. But seeing Spike already there made things clearer, and I crept back out to the den and eased onto the couch. I curled up beneath a small lap blanket and only then exhaled, breathing very carefully.

When I awoke stiff and guilty the next morning, Lois and Spike were gone. Some time around midafternoon, she came home alone. She was wearing a pair of my old torn jeans and a baggy flannel shirt and a Braves cap pulled down over her eyes. We didn't speak. I went out into the garage and cleaned out junk that had been there for a couple of years, hauled it off to the dump in the truck, then came in and showered. I smelled something delicious cooking in the kitchen. When I'd dressed and come out of the bedroom, the house was lighted only by a soft flickering from the dining room. Lois sat at her end of the table alone, eating. She paid me no attention as I stood in the doorway.

"Lois," I said. "Where's Spike?"

She cut a piece of pork roast and chewed for a moment. Her hair was wet and combed straight back off her forehead. She wore eye makeup, bringing out the depth and what I have only a few times truly recognized as the astonishing beauty of her deep green eyes. Her polished nails glistened in the candlelight.

The table was set with our good china and silver and a very nice meal. She seemed like someone I'd only now just met, whom I'd walked in on by her own design. She looked at me, and my heart sank, and the knot that had formed in my chest the night before began to dissolve into sorrow.

"He was getting pretty old," she said. She took a sip of wine, which was an expensive bottle we'd saved for a special occasion. "I had him put to sleep."

I'M SURPRISED AT HOW OFTEN DOGS MAKE THE NEWS. There was the one about the dog elected mayor of a town in California. And another about a dog that could play the piano, I believe he was a schnauzer. More often, though, they're involved in criminal cases—dog bitings, dog pack attacks on children. I've seen several stories about dogs who shoot their masters. There was one of these in the stack of old *Mobile Registers* in the front room. "Dog Shoots, Kills Master," the headline read. Way back in '59. How could you not read a story like that? The man carried his shotguns in his car. He stopped to talk to his relative on the road, and let the dogs run. When his relative left, the man called his dogs. One of them jumped into the backseat and hit the trigger on a gun, which discharged and struck him "below the stomach," the article said. The man hollered to his relative, "I'm shot!" and fell over in the ditch.

There was another article called "Death Row Dog," about a dog that had killed so many cats in his neighborhood that a judge sentenced him to death. And another one sentenced to be moved to the country or die, just because he barked so much. There was another one like that just this year, about a condemned biter that won a last-minute reprieve. I'm told in medieval times animals were regularly put on trial, with witnesses and testimony and so forth. But it is relatively rare today.

One story, my favorite, was headlined "Dog Lady Claims Close Encounter." It was about an old woman who lived alone with about forty-two dogs. Strays were drawn to her house, whereupon they disappeared from the streets forever. At night, when sirens passed on the streets of the town, a great howling rose from inside her walls. Then one day, the dogs' barking kept on and on, raising a racket like they'd never done before. It went on all day, all that night, and was still going the next day. People passing the house on the sidewalk heard things slamming against the doors, saw dog claws scratching at the windowpanes, teeth gnawing at the sashes. Finally, the police broke in. Dogs burst through the open door never to be seen again. Trembling skeletons, who wouldn't eat their own kind, crouched in the corners, behind chairs. Dog shit everywhere, the stench was awful. They found dead dogs in the basement freezer, little shit dogs whole and bigger ones cut up into parts. Police started looking around for the woman's gnawed-up corpse, but she was nowhere to be found.

At first they thought the starving dogs had eaten her up: clothes, skin, hair, muscle, and bone. But then, four days later, some hunters found her wandering naked out by a reservoir, all scratched up, disoriented.

She'd been abducted, she said, and described tall creatures with the heads of dogs, who licked her hands and sniffed her privates.

"They took me away in their ship," she said. "On the dog star, it's them that owns us. These here," she said, sweeping her arm about to indicate Earth, "they ain't nothing compared to them dogs."

ON A WARM AFTERNOON IN NOVEMBER, A BEAUTIFUL breezy Indian summer day, the wind steered Lois somehow in her Volkswagen up to the house. She'd been driving around. I got a couple of beers from the fridge and we sat out back sipping them, not talking. Then we sat there looking at each other for a little while. We drank a couple more beers. A rosy sun ticked down behind the old grove on the far side of the field and light softened, began to blue. The dogs' tails moved like periscopes through the tall grass.

"Want to walk?" I said.

"Okay."

The dogs trotted up as we climbed through the barbed-wire fence, then bounded ahead, leaping like deer over stands of grass. Lois stopped out in the middle of the field and slipped her hands in the pockets of my jeans.

"I missed you," she said. She shook her head. "I sure as hell didn't want to."

"Well," I said. "I know." Anger over Spike rose in me then, but I held my tongue. "I missed you, too," I said. She looked at me with anger and desire.

We knelt down. I rolled in the grass, flattening a little bed. We attacked each other. Kissing her, I felt like I wanted to eat her alive. I took big soft bites of her breasts, which were heavy and smooth. She gripped my waist with her nails, pulled hard at me, kicked my ass with her heels, and bit my shoulders, and when she came she pulled my hair so hard I cried out. After we'd caught our breath, she pushed me off of her like a sack of feed corn.

We lay on our backs. The sky was empty. It was all we could see, with the grass so high around us. We didn't talk for a while, and then Lois began to tell me what had happened at the vet's. She told me how she'd held Spike while the vet gave him the injection.

"I guess he just thought he was getting more shots," she said. "Like when I first took him in."

She said Spike was so good, he didn't fight it. He looked at her when she placed her hands on him to hold him down. He was frightened, and didn't wag his tail. And she was already starting to cry, she said. The vet asked her if she was sure this was what she wanted to do. She nodded her head. He gave Spike the shot.

She was crying as she told me this.

"He laid down his head and closed his eyes," she said. "And then, with my hands on him like that, I tried to pull him back to me. Back to us." She said, No, Spike, don't go. She pleaded with him not to die. The vet was upset and said some words to her and left the room in anger, left her alone in her grief. And when it was over, she had a sense of not knowing where she was for a moment. Sitting on the floor in there alone with the strong smell of flea killer and antiseptic, and the white of the floor and walls and the stainless steel of the examination table where Spike had died and where he lay now, and in that moment he was everything she had ever loved.

She drained the beer can, wiping her eyes. She took a deep breath and let it out slowly. "I just wanted to hurt you. I didn't realize how much it would hurt me."

She shook her head.

"And now I can't forgive you," she said. "Or me."

In the old days when Harold was still with Westley and I was still with Lois, Harold had thrown big cookout parties. He had a pit we'd dug for slow-cooking whole pigs, a brick grill for chickens, and a smoker made from an old oil drum. So one crisp evening late in bird season, to reestablish some of the old joy of life, Harold set up another one and a lot of our old friends and acquaintances came. Then Phelan showed up, drunk, with the head of a pig he'd bought at the slaughterhouse. He'd heard you could buy the head of a pig and after an afternoon at the Blind Horse he thought it would be interesting to bring one to the barbecue. He insisted on putting it into the smoker, so it would have made a scene to stop him. Every half hour or so, he opened the lid with a flourish and checked the head. The pig's eyelids shrank and opened halfway, the eyes turned translucent. Its hide leaked beaded moisture and turned a doughy pale. People lost their appetites. Many became quiet and left. "I'm sorry," Phelan stood on the porch and announced as they left, stood there like Marc Antony in Shakespeare. "No need to go. I've come to bury this pig, not to eat him."

Finally Harold took the pig's head from the smoker and threw it out onto the far edge of the yard, and Phelan stood over it a minute, reciting some lines from Tennyson. Ike and Otis went sniffing up, sniffing, their eyes like brown marbles. They backed off and sat just outside of the porch light and watched the pig's head steaming in the grass as if it had dropped screaming through the atmosphere and plopped into the yard, an alien thing, now cooling, a new part of the landscape, a new mystery evolving, a new thing in the world, there whenever they rounded the corner, still there, stinking and mute, until Harold buried it out in the field. After that we pretty much kept to ourselves.

We passed our winter boarded up in the house, the cracks beneath doors and around windows and in the walls stuffed with old horse blankets and newspaper and wads of clothing falling apart at the seams, the space heaters hissing in the tall-ceilinged rooms. We went out for whiskey and dry goods and meat, occasionally stopped by the Blind Horse of an early afternoon, but spent our evenings at home. We wrote letters to those we loved and missed and planned spring reunions when possible. Harold's once-illicit lover, Sophia the surveyor, came by a few times. I wrote Lois, but received no reply. I wrote to my editor at the *Journal* and asked to return in the late spring, but it may be that I should move on.

It is March just now, when the ancients sacrificed young dogs and men to the crop and mixed the blood with the corn. Harold is thinking of planting some beans. We've scattered the astonished heads of bream in the soil, mourning doves in their beautiful lidded repose. The blood of the birds and the fishes, and the seeds of the harvest. I found the skin of our resident chicken snake, shed and left on the hearth. He's getting ready to move outside. The days are warming, and though it's still cool in the evenings we stay out late in the backyard, sipping Harold's Famous Grouse to stay warm, trying in our hearts to restore a little order to the world. I'm hoping to be out here at least until midnight, when Canis Major finally descends in the west, having traveled of an evening across the southern horizon. It rises up before sunset and glows bright above the pastures at dusk, big bright Sirius the first star in the sky, to wish upon for a fruitful planting. It stirs me to look up at them, all of them, not just this one, stirs me beyond my own enormous sense of personal disappointment. And Harold, in his cups, calls Otis over and strikes a pose: "Orion, the hunter," he says, "and his Big Dog." Otis, looking up at him, strikes the pose, too: Is there something out there? Will we hunt? Harold holds the pose, and Otis trots out into the field, restless, snuffling. I can feel the earth turning beneath us, rolling beneath the stars. Looking up, I lose my balance and fall back flat in the grass.

If the Grouse lasts we'll stay out till dawn, when the stellar dog and hunter are off tracing the histories of other worlds, the cold distant figures of the hero Perseus and his love Andromeda fading in the morning glow into nothing.

And then we will stumble into the falling-down house and to our beds. And all our dreams will roll toward the low point in the center of the house and pool there together, mingling in the drafts under the doors with last year's crumbling leaves and the creeping skinks and the dreams of the dogs, who must dream of the chase, the hunt, of bitches in heat, the mingling of old spoors with their own musty odors. And deep in sleep they dream of space travel, of dancing on their hind legs, of being men with the heads and muzzles of dogs, of sleeping in beds with sheets, of driving cars, of taking their fur coats off each night and making love face to face. Of cooking their food. And Harold and I dream of days of following the backs of men's knees, and faint trails in the soil, the overpowering odors of all our kin, our pasts, every mistake as strong as sulfur, our victories lingering traces here and there. The house is disintegrating into dust. The end of all of this is near.

Just yesterday Harold went into the kitchen for coffee and found the chicken snake curled around the warm pot. Otis went wild. Harold whooped. The screams of Sophia the surveyor rang high and clear and regular, and in my half-sleep I could only imagine the source of this dissonance filling the air. Oh, slay me and scatter my parts in the field. The house was hell. And Ike, too, baying—out on the porch—full-lunged, without memory or sense, with only the barking of Otis to clue his continuing: already lost within his own actions, forgetting his last conscious needs.

SEEING EYE

THE DOG CAME TO THE CURB'S EDGE AND STOPPED. The man holding on to his halter stopped beside him. Across the street, the signal flashed the words "Don't Walk." The dog saw the signal but paid little notice. He was trained to see what mattered: the absence of moving traffic. The signal kept blinking. The cars kept driving through the intersection. He watched the cars, listened to the intensity of their engines, the arid whine of their tires. He listened for something he'd become accustomed to hearing, the buzz and tumbling of switches from the box on the pole next to them. The dog associated it with the imminent stopping of the cars. He looked back over his right shoulder at the man, who stood with his head cocked, listening to the traffic.

A woman behind them spoke up.

"Huh," she said. "The light's stuck."

The dog looked at her, then turned back to watch the traffic, which continued to rush through the intersection without pause.

"I'm going down a block," the woman said. She spoke to the man. "Would you like me to show you a detour? No telling how long this light will be."

"No, thank you," the man said. "We'll just wait a little bit. Right, Buck?" The dog looked back over his shoulder at the man, then watched the woman walk away.

"Good luck," the woman said. The dog's ears stood up and he stiffened for just a second.

"She said 'luck,' not 'Buck,' " the man said, laughing easily and reaching down to scratch the dog's ears. He gripped the loose skin on Buck's neck with his right hand and gave it an affectionate shake. He continued to hold the halter guide loosely with his left.

The dog watched the traffic rush by.

"We'll just wait here, Buck," the man said. "By the time we go a block out of our way, the light will've fixed itself." He cleared his throat and cocked his head, as if listening for something. The dog dipped his head and shifted his shoulders in the halter.

The man laughed softly.

"If we went down a block, I'll bet that light would get stuck, too. We'd be following some kind of traveling glitch across town. We could go for miles, and then end up in some field, and a voice saying, 'I suppose you're wondering why I've summoned you here.' "

It was the longest they'd ever stood waiting for traffic to stop. The dog saw people across the street wait momentarily, glance around, then leave. He watched the traffic. It began to have a hypnotic effect upon him: the traffic, the blinking crossing signal. His focus on the next move, the crossing, on the implied courses of the pedestrians around them and those still waiting at the opposite curb, on the potential obstructions ahead, dissolved into the rare luxury of wandering attention.

The sounds of the traffic grinding through the intersection were diminished to a small aural dot in the back of his mind, and he became aware of the regular bleat of a slow-turning box fan in an open window of the building behind them. Odd scents distinguished themselves in his nostrils and blended into a rich funk that swirled about the pedestrians who stopped next to them, a secret aromatic history that eddied about him even as the pedestrians muttered among themselves and moved on.

The hard clean smell of new shoe leather seeped from the air-conditioned stores, overlaying the drift of worn leather and grime that eased from tiny musty pores in the sidewalk. He snuffled at them and sneezed. In a trembling confusion he was aware of all that was carried in the breeze, the strong odor of tobacco and the sharp rake of its smoke, the gasoline and exhaust fumes and the stench of aging rubber, the fetid waves that rolled through it all from garbage bins in the alleys and on the backstreet curbs.

He lowered his head and shifted his shoulders in the harness like a boxer.

"Easy, Buck," the man said.

Sometimes in their room the man paced the floor and seemed to say his words in time with his steps until he became like a lulling clock to Buck as he lay resting beneath the dining table. He dozed to the man's mumbling and the sifting sound of his fingers as they grazed the pages of his book. At times in their dark room the man sat on the edge of his cot and scratched Buck's ears and spoke to him. "Panorama, Buck," he would say. "That's the most difficult to recall. I can see the details, with my hands, with my nose, my tongue. It brings them back. But the big picture. I feel like I must be replacing it with something phony, like a Disney movie or something." Buck looked up at the man's shadowed face in the dark room, at his small eyes in their sallow depressions.

On the farm where he'd been raised before his training at the school, Buck's name had been Pete. The children and the old man and the woman had tussled with him, thrown sticks, said, "Pete! Good old Pete." They called out to him, mumbled the name into his fur. But now the man always said "Buck" in the same tone of voice, soft and gentle. As if the man were speaking to himself. As if Buck were not really there.

"I miss colors, Buck," the man would say. "It's getting harder to remember them. The blue planet. I remember that. Pictures from space. From out in the blackness."

Looking up from the intersection, Buck saw birds

dart through the sky between buildings as quickly as they slipped past the open window at dawn. He heard their high-pitched cries so clearly that he saw their beady eyes, their barbed tongues flicking between parted beaks. He salivated at the dusky taste of a dove once he'd held in his mouth. And in his most delicate bones he felt the murmur of some incessant activity, the low hum beyond the visible world. His hackles rose and his muscles tingled with electricity.

There was a metallic whirring, like a big fat June bug stuck on its back, followed by the dull clunk of the switch in the traffic control box. Cars stopped. The lane opened up before them, and for a moment no one moved, as if the empty-eyed vehicles were not to be trusted, restrained only by some fragile miracle of faith. He felt the man carefully regrip the leather harness. He felt the activity of the world spool down into the tight and rifled tunnel of their path.

"Forward, Buck," said the man.

He leaned into the harness and moved them into the world.

AGNES OF BOB

AGNES MENKEN, MISSING HER LEFT EYE, AND BOB the bulldog, missing his right, often sat together on their porch, Agnes in her straight-backed rocking chair and Bob in her lap. Together they could see anything coming, Bob to one side and Agnes to the other. They always seemed to be staring straight ahead but really they were looking both ways.

Whereas Bob's bad right eye was sewn up, Agnes had a false one that roved. It was obvious to her that people often had trouble telling which eye was the good one, so sometimes she would look at them awhile with the good one, and then when they'd become comfortable with this she switched and looked at them with the false one, which was clear and had the direct hard-bearing frankness of detachment. In her good eye's peripheral vision she could see the general distress that this caused.

Despite his years and his sewn-up eye, Bob was as stout and fit as a young dog. He stayed that way naturally, as dogs of his type will, having the metabolism of all small muscular animals. He was tight, compact—much like her late husband, Pops, but just the opposite of Agnes, who was lanky. Officially, he had been Pops's dog, the son he'd never had, she supposed. In that way Agnes had felt at best like a stepmother, standing just a little apart. Pops and Bob had understood one another, shared a language of some kind that only they'd understood, whereas Agnes could never tell if Bob was listening to her or not.

Nevertheless, she and Bob had become closer in the year since Pops had died. They had their routine together. Bob ate twice a day, morning and evening. He got to stay outside in the fenced backyard as long as he wanted during the day. At night he slept on Agnes's bed, down near the footboard. And every evening, once early and once late, she let him out to pee in the yard. A neighbor wandered out back to look at the moon would see the light on her back porch snap on, the door creak open, see Bob come flying out onto the grass, snarling and grunting the way Boston bulldogs do, dashing around in the dark near the back of the yard. But Agnes hadn't the patience with him Pops'd had, how Pops would sit at the kitchen table smoking, sipping coffee, waiting till Bob sauntered back up to the door and barked to be let back in. Now, Bob would hardly have time to pee before the door creaked open on its hinges again and Agnes started in on him, saying, "Where are you? What are you doing back there? Go on, now. Go on and do what you're gonna do. What are you doing? Come on. Come on in here and finish up your supper. I want to go to bed. Come on in this door. Where are you? Please, Bob. I'm tired, boy. What are you doing out there? Come on in here. Come on. Come on." Then Bob would stop, sniff around, shoot a quick stream into the monkey grass, lob a fading arc to the bark of the popcorn tree, and then leap back into the light of the porch. And she would pull the door shut, turn all three of the dead bolts, snap off the kitchen light, and feel her way along the hallway to bed.

EXCEPT FOR THE HOUSE NEXT DOOR ON HER EAST SIDE, where the professor lived with his wife and two little girls, this seemed to Agnes like a neighborhood of widows. Next door on the west side was Lura Campbell, eighty-four, who insisted on driving every day. She did all right once she got out of her azalea-lined driveway, but she had the worst time trying to back herself out. On this morning, Agnes lay in bed and listened to Lura's old Impala wheeze to a start, clank into Reverse, back up a little ways, and then *screee*, into the azaleas. Clank clank, into Drive, pull forward. Clank clank, into Reverse, back up. *Screee*, into the azaleas. Clank clank, into Drive, pull forward. Clank clank, into Reverse, back up. *Screee*, into the azaleas. All the way down her driveway. Drove Agnes crazy. She'd said to Lura, I don't see why you feel like you got to get out and go every morning. Well, I like to go, Lura said. I don't see any sense in going just to be going, Agnes said. Well, Lura said, I just have to get out and go somewhere, I can't sit here at the house.

Agnes did not want to end up like Lura, an aimless, doddering wanderer driving down the middle of the street in her ancient automobile threatening dogs and children. She hoped that something would happen to ease her on out of the world before she got that way, that she would die in her sleep or simply somehow disappear, whisked into thin air by the hand of God. She had made her peace with God, though she'd never liked religion. She certainly wasn't afraid of God, like she had been once without realizing it. She would face God like she would anybody else, with dignity and demanding a little respect in return. She'd never willingly offended God, had only ignored Him a little, like everyone else. But recently she had silently said, If it comes a time when it's convenient to You, go ahead.

She thought, Maybe I'll see Pops, and with two good eyes.

She fished her glass one out of the little dish of solution on the bedside table, popped it in, and eased her legs off the side of the bed. As soon as her toes touched the cool bare floor, Bob was there, leaping into the air around her like a circus dog.

"Get," she waved at him, shuffling into the kitchen to make coffee. "Get."

The coffee made, she poured a cup, took it out to the porch, and no sooner had her bottom touched the chair than Bob jumped into her lap, circled, and settled in his sphinxlike pose to observe the traffic.

Carolyn Barr and April Ready walked briskly by, swinging their arms like majorettes. They waved, Agnes nodded. The women, in their sixties, had the legs of thirty-year-olds.

"Amazing, Bob," Agnes muttered. "I bet I know why their old boys kicked off."

She and Pops had had what she'd considered a normal life, in that regard. Toward the end, Pops got to where he wasn't interested, and she didn't mind, much. The truth was, they'd never really gotten over the embarrassment. She'd always figured more sex would've been a good thing, but she'd never brought it up with Pops. It seemed frivolous. They'd never talked about sex, never even used the word. She'd always worked, just like him. Forty years! Forty years at the power company for her. He'd kept books at the steam feed works, never retired. A chain-smoker with Coke-bottle-thick glasses, he came home smoking, seemed like steam from the works leaking out of his thick windows onto the world. When he had his attack, he fell into a pile of foundry sand and suffocated.

The day Pops had died, the widow Louella Marshall (a Baptist) had come by. Her husband, Herbert, had been dead for ten years, and since then she hadn't so much as had coffee with a man. She'd married her church, is what she said. Agnes couldn't stand her because she seemed so smug, and Agnes couldn't believe she wasn't a phony, a religious bully who was scared to death of dying herself, afraid she was going to hell for having secretly wished her bullying husband would die and leave her alone. Agnes wasn't afraid of going to hell, but when Louella sat in her armchair and made like to comfort her by saying God had taken Pops to be with Him in heaven, she had gotten so angry she took her coffee cup and saucer into the kitchen and dashed them in the sink. She didn't pretend to have dropped them.

After that, for a while, she frequently had a dream in which she was swimming out in the middle of the ocean, strong as one of those nuts that used to swim across the English Channel. But then there was a roaring sound, and she'd look up and see it was the edge of the world, and a beast would rise up with the body of a dragon and the face of Pops, which then changed into the dog face of Bob, and she awoke in her bedroom where the blue night-light made the damp air seem like water and the breeze through the window sounded like ocean swells and it took her some minutes to calm down and hear Bob down at the foot of her bed, grunting and thrashing in some dream of his own.

She had realized then that she was afraid of dying, and afraid of what had happened to Pops. But she could not be like Louella and believe that this was God's will, that he had singled out Pops like an assassin. She decided that she would face the possibility of her own death with dignity, by inviting it in, leaving the door unlocked, and that in that way she would be in charge and unafraid. We all know death better than we think, she said to herself.

The only one who'd said anything interesting on that day at her house had been poor Lura Campbell, who had sat tiny and quiet on Agnes's huge old sofa and sipped her coffee and said, when there'd been a long quiet spell in the room, "I think if I had it to do all over again, after Lester passed away, I'da done some traveling."

Louella Marshall said, "Well, Lura, where in the world would you've gone? To Florida?"

"Oh, I don't know," Lura said. "I'da just got into my car and gone."

Lura and her car.

AGNES DIDN'T SOCIALIZE WITH ANY OF THE WIDOWS. SHE tended the yard and looked after Bob and kept the house fairly clean and watched for rare birds at her feeders. She didn't see many rare birds, which was natural seeing as how they *were* rare, but the occasional chickadee or purple finch made it interesting enough.

Warm days, she sunned in her lounge chair on the patio out back, her eyes shut tight against the glare and the heat, talking to Bob the whole time. She could hear him grunting and snuffling and rooting around like a hog. Whenever he was quiet she raised up and looked, to see if anyone had walked up, and then lay back down. She hated sunbathing, but it was good for the psoriasis, and it helped fight her natural pallor, which made her feel like those little cave frogs she'd seen once on a trip to the mountains with Pops. Little red eyes and the rest of them clear as a jellyfish, you could see their little hearts pumping and their veins jumping, like their skins were made of glass.

Sometimes she volunteered to take the little girls next door to the pool. Swimming was good for her, the doctor said, and Agnes had always liked the water. She wasn't much on the surface, since she was too slim to float, but she liked to be underwater, moving along in steady breaststrokes like a long slow fish. She liked the look of things underwater, the silent and bright world that seemed strange in the way that a dream is, very intimate and distant at the same time.

After a swim, lying in the sun beside the pool was easier than tanning in her buggy backyard with Bob always snorting around. She'd take a brush and brush her wet hair straight back and forget about it. She couldn't do anything with it anymore, it was getting so thin and frizzy. The gray she didn't care about. She pretty much let Sherilyn just chop it short and do it up in a little permanent. She got it washed once a week. She knew short hair made her neck look longer, but there wasn't any way around that. Her good eye was a little smaller than the false one and a little reddened from strain, her nose was a little long, and her back was bent just a little forward because of less than ideal posture. She could see this when she walked past a storefront window and saw her reflection. Now, to boot, her fingers were swollen with a mild arthritis and there were the faded, healed reminders of a few small sores on her arms and legs from the psoriasis. It was a good thing she never cared much about appearances. And after a swim, with her muscles tingling from the exercise, she cared even less.

Nevertheless, a tan seemed to help all of that, and helped create a natural vigor, and in her mind's eye she sought a dignity in the way she looked and mentally compared herself to a tall gray crane beside a bay or a lake, and she tried to carry herself with that dignity in mind. She walked slowly and deliberately, like a crane, and without thinking kept her eye fixed that way, like they did when they were fishing or just stalking along.

IT WAS A NATURAL COMPARISON, GIVEN HER INTEREST IN birds and the three feeders she kept in her backyard.

"Look at that, Bob," she'd say. "I believe that's a towhee pecking around down there." Bob stared at her, jaws clamped. Then he let his tongue out again and started panting.

She sometimes forgot it was Pops who'd first started watching the birds. Feeding them, anyway. He built the feeders in his shop out in the garage. Then he started to read about them a little, and he'd keep track of when they came and went, and he'd sit with her in the kitchen sipping coffee and looking out at the feeders in the spring and announce their arrivals from Argentina, Paraguay, Brazil, and Venezuela, Peru and Colombia and Costa Rica. "Flown here nonstop from the Yucatan," he'd say. "Made a little stop down on the coast."

And he took her down there one time in the season. They put on their sun gear, light long-sleeved shirts and khaki pants and tennis shoes and light socks, broad hats, sunglasses and binoculars. They drove down the beach road to the old fort and camped out for two days on the grounds with a bunch of odd ones who called themselves birders and walked the sandy trails and Pops made notes in a little spiral-bound notebook.

One day they were standing on the beach and birds started to fall out of the sky.

"Oh," one of the birders cried, "it's a tanager fall-out." A momentary alarm shook Agnes, naturally associating the word with its nuclear meaning. But then she caught on, birds plopping to the white sand all around them. Bright red birds with black wings and black tails, and dull yellow birds amongst them.

They'd stood still, as had all the others for some minutes, and then people began to get down on their hands and knees and take close-up pictures of the birds, who were too exhausted to move another feather. People picked them up and stroked them and set them back down. Before they could stop him, Bob—who'd cautiously sniffed at one bird—began taking them into his jaws and dropping them at her and Pops's feet like gifts. Some of the birders got upset and started hollering like fools until Pops got Bob back on the leash and kept him from retrieving any more tanagers.

"He ain't a retriever," Pops said later. "He's built for killing small animals. He knows we like the birds, I guess."

That day, Agnes had stood there, the startling scarlet birds falling around her, and listened to the surf bashing at the sand, and she could see the churning tidal struggle down at the point, at the mouth of the bay. She looked out over the Gulf and thought about the birds having crossed all that water without even a rest, and she thought about the fishes and other creatures that traveled beneath those waters, strong and free as they pleased, roaming without the boundaries of continents or countries or cities and towns or jobs or houses or yards, and the idea of the freedom of such a journey stirred in her something like joy and something like frustration. She didn't know what to do with it, this feeling, and she felt so strange standing amidst these people struck wild with wonder over the tanager fallout while all she could feel was the most curious detachment from it all.

SHE DECIDED SHE NEEDED TO GO TO THE POOL AND ON A whim thought it'd be nice to drive Lura over there with her. If Lura liked so much to *go*, then she'd give her somewhere to go *to*. She knew Lura wouldn't swim, but it might be nice for her to sit in the shade and watch the others. Agnes put her swimsuit on and slipped a slightly faded sundress over it, got into her sandals and sunglasses, and went over to fetch Lura.

Lura was sitting in her automatic chair and she fumbled for the button, pushed it, and the chair began to rise slowly until it slid Lura out onto the floor on her feet and then sat there like a sproinged jack-in-the-box while Lura went into the kitchen to get Agnes a bowl of homemade ice cream.

"I don't want any ice cream," Agnes said. "Let's get in my car and go over to the swimming pool."

"I made this cream last week and it's still good, but I can't eat it all," Lura said.

"I thought," Agnes said loudly then, thinking maybe Lura didn't have her hearing aid in, "that I would give you some*place* to *go*, instead of just wandering. And you wouldn't have to drive."

"Well, I like to drive," Lura said, fiddling in her silverware drawer. "I can drive just fine."

"I didn't say you *couldn't* drive, Lura. I just thought you might like to go someplace with *me*."

"Well, I can drive us to the pool," Lura said, like someone who'd been insulted.

Agnes felt her stomach knot up just thinking about riding with Lura, but she could see what this was turning into and went on out and got into Lura's car and rolled down her window. After what must have been a quarter of an hour, Lura finally came down her back-porch steps wearing a light cotton dress with a floral print and carrying a wide, floppy garden hat that looked like a collapsed sombrero. She put the hat onto the seat between them and got in behind the giant steering wheel of the Impala. She looked like a child driving a city bus, Agnes thought.

Then Lura began her driving ritual. She pulled on her white cotton gloves and fished her keys out of her purse, chose the proper key, and inserted it into the ignition. She pumped the accelerator pedal one time with the toe of her Hush Puppy, then turned the key. The old engine turned over once, coughed, then died with a hydraulic sigh. Lura pumped again, turned the key, the engine wheezed once, caught, and Lura held her foot down until the car roared like a dump truck. She let it die back, and gently pulled the gear stick down into Reverse. The transmission made its familiar clanking noise, Agnes felt the bump of the car into gear, and Lura placed both gloved hands on the wheel and peered into the rearview mirror as she began her journey out of her driveway. Obliquely, and true to her lights, she leaned the Impala's right fender into her pink azaleas, and the thin and agonized atonal chorus of stems against paint and metal began.

"Oh, Lord," Agnes muttered. "Here we go."

Clank clank, into Drive, Lura pulled forward. Clank clank, into Reverse.

"Lura," Agnes said. *"Lura."* Lura pressed on the brake pedal and looked at her.

"Why don't you use the *side* mirror," Agnes said.

Lura looked at her blankly.

"If you just keep your left fender close to the bushes on that side, you'll be all right," Agnes said.

Lura said, "I couldn't see the rest of the car if I did that."

"You don't have to see the whole car," Agnes said. "Can you see the whole car when you're moving ahead? If you keep it close to the bushes on your side, the other side will take care of itself."

"I do all right," Lura said. "Well, I can't use the side mirror, I never have."

"Lura, it's just easier," Agnes started to say, but Lura's toe had strayed from the brake pedal and the car's high idle propelled them backwards. Agnes, looking into the mirror on her side, thought for a moment that they would make it clear out of the driveway and into the street by accident, but then Lura realized what was happening and yanked the wheel, and the car jumped the curb and plowed into the bank of azaleas with a paint-rending screech. Lura kept one hand on the gearshift, pulled the stick clank clank into Drive, and the car shot forward into the driveway and jerked to a stop.

"Look at that," Lura said, disgusted. "Agnes, will you just let me drive?"

In the end, Agnes got out and waited on the sidewalk until Lura had gotten the car into the street. Then she got in and they drove at Lura's steady fifteen-miles-per-hour pace to the pool.

Lura took a couple of spaces near the gate, put the broad straw garden hat back onto her head, and they walked on in.

"Well, here we are," Lura said. "You go on in. I'll just find somewhere to sit down."

"I'm going to get some sun before I swim," Agnes said. "Why don't you sit over there under that awning and get yourself some ice tea? I'll take one of those loungers over there and stretch out."

"Well, that sounds good," Lura said. "I don't see how you can stand that sun. I'm glad I wore my hat. *Whew.*" She adjusted the hat and began working her fingers out of the white cotton gloves as she made her way over to the refreshment area.

Agnes walked down to the deck behind the diving boards, spread her Panama City Beach beach towel onto one of the cedar chaise longues, and eased herself down. This was the last time she'd ever go anywhere with Lura. Lord, what an old biddy. She decided not to fool with the suntan lotion. She hoped Lura wouldn't wander off and strand her, or worse yet totter off and fall into the pool and drown. She decided to alert the lifeguard to that possibility. He was a strong-looking boy and very capable, she was sure. She looked at him, sitting up in his high chair, twirling his silver whistle.

She got up and went over to the chair.

"Young man?" she said.

The lifeguard looked down at her. He wore black sunglasses and she couldn't see his eyes.

"Yes, ma'am," he said.

"Would you keep an eye on that elderly lady over at the refreshment stand? I'm afraid she might wander off and fall into the pool."

The lifeguard looked down at her for a moment, then over in Lura's direction.

"The lady with the big hat and the sunglasses, ma'am?"

Agnes looked and saw that Lura had pulled out her pair of giant, squared geriatric sunglasses and put them on.

"That's her," she said.

"Yes'm," the lifeguard said, "I'll keep an eye on her."

She looked up at him a moment longer as he put the silver whistle to his lips and blew two short notes, like a songbird's call, and nodded to some action out in the pool. He looked like a Greek god on the mount, like Neptune.

"I thank you," Agnes said, and went back to her lounge chair. Students from the college lay on their towels along the pool's edge. It was very hot, and every now and then one of the girls got up and stepped down the pool ladder into the water, holding her hair up on top of her head, until the water touched the back of her neck, then climbed out of the water, still holding her hair. Some girls liked to wet their heads, arching their necks back and lowering their long straight hair into the pool. The boys behind their dark glasses watched the girls lower themselves into the pool and emerge with water sparkling on their oiled bodies, then watched them walk to their towels again.

Agnes watched them all. They were all very nearly naked and all brown as the glazed doughnuts Pops used to bring home from Shipley's on Sunday mornings after his early drive to smoke his Sunday cigar. She thought about the students having sex, she knew they all did these days, and wondered if they had to get to know one another before they did it or if they just did it casual as dogs, without a thought. She remembered the taste of the hot soft doughnuts Pops would bring home and it made her so restless she sat up straight in the lounge chair.

Lura was still in the shade at the refreshment stand, fanning herself with a magazine. Agnes got up and eased herself over the pool's edge, let go, and sank to the bottom.

The water sent a great shock of cool through her body. She felt immersed in a great big glass of ice water. She looked around. Everything was green and bright. Way off down at the other end someone dove in and swam across, just thrashing arms and legs. She could see the legs of children dancing around at the shallow end. A cloud sailed over, made all jumpy by the waves. She could see people walk along the pool's edge, their bodies broken into pieces and quivering like Jell-O. The legs and bottom and shoulders and one arm of a girl came slowly down the ladder and slowly climbed back out, jerking like something big outside the water was taking her bite by bite. Agnes felt fine not breathing, as if there was a great supply of air in her lungs. She'd always had wonderful lung capacity. At some point, she thought, it seemed like a body would simply stop needing to take in so much air, stop needing to breathe all the time. Another girl came partially down the ladder, dipped her long hair back into the pool, and then walked back up into the air. Agnes felt as if they all belonged to another world, too thin and insubstantial to sustain her, and the one she was in, her world here deep in the clear green water, was much more pleasurable, much more peaceful. She remembered a dream, swimming in the ocean in a vast school of swift metallic fish, their eyes all around her, the feeling she got eye to eye with the fishes, and their effortless speed and flashing tails. She felt something stir in her, growing, until she felt filled with it. Her chest ached with it. Saturday nights, Pops would cook their meals. He loved to fry fish. Take Bob out to the lake and get on a bream bed. Pops would come home with a stringer, a mess, wet fish flopping and mouths groping for air. Made her chest ache, watching them. Pops would clean the bream out back, throw Bob a fish head. Bob tossing fish heads around the yard like balls. She was on the brink of a wonderful vision, as if in a moment she would know what Pops had seen as he passed through his own heart and a pile of washed foundry sand into the next world.

She thought she heard the distant trill of a bird and looked up as a crash of bubbles shot down from the surface. The bubbles cleared and she saw it was the lifeguard, his dark and curly hair about his face like a nest of water serpents. His eyes were a clear blue revelation, open wide and upon her. She held out her arms. He came forward and held her and pulled her gently upward. Her hands felt the muscles moving powerfully along his back. She thought that he must have wings, this angel, and he would take her on some beautiful journey.

AGNES LAY IN HER LAWN CHAIR, WATCHING THE LAST RAYS of the afternoon sift through tiny gaps between the leaves. The light shifted in an almost kaleidoscopic fashion as the leaves trembled in a breeze that seemed an augury of the evening. She did not fear them, the passing of the day nor the coming of the evening. She had never felt so relaxed or open to the world around her.

On the way home, Lura's words had been as distant and melodic as a birdsong. The drive had taken only seconds. Lura must have been driving all of thirty-five.

She heard Lura now, as she leaned over Agnes's lawn chair to look at her.

"I imagine you've had enough sun," Lura said. "You're addled. I'm lucky I'm not dead of a heart attack, you nearly scared me to death."

Bob ran full-speed in broad circles around the yard just inside the fence. He stopped and stood rigid beside the monkey grass patch beneath the pecan tree, then leaped stiff-legged into the middle of it. He thrashed around and came tearing out of it as if something were after him. A few feet away he stopped, turned around, and barked at it.

"Be quiet, Bob," Agnes said. Bob looked back at her, as if measuring her authority.

"You ought to let me take you to the doctor, anyway," Lura said. "You nearly drowned."

"I was all right."

"I don't know how you can say that. That boy had to pull you out of the water like an old log." She touched her hair. "I've left my hat."

"Lura, just sit down and be quiet or go home. I'm feeling so peaceful."

"You've had a near-death experience," Lura said.

"Oh, be quiet," Agnes said. Lura touched her hair again, started to say something, then sat down in a lawn chair, and Agnes again turned her attention to the sunset coloring the light behind the trees. The light deepened and the breeze ran through the leaves like the passing of a gentle hand. Agnes didn't know when she had felt so much at peace. It had not been her time to go. But she had been close enough to see into that moment, and she did not dislike what she had seen.

The bank of orange clouds behind and above the treeline began to fade into slate against the deepening blue of the sky. The loud and raucous birds of the day had retreated, and the quiet of evening began to settle in. The light faded measurably, moment by moment. It was so beautiful she did not think she was not seeing it with two eyes. She heard Bob and looked for him against the purpling green of the lawn and the shrubbery. He'd begun again his racing around and around. He'd worn a narrow path in the grass, a perfect oval like a racetrack. She found him, a speeding, blurred ball of black and white led by a wild and wide-open eye, and watched as he zipped past and approached the far fence. And then, in violation of what had seemed a perfect order, he suddenly leaped. He leaped amazingly high, and with great velocity. He leaped, as if launched by a giant invisible spring in the grass, or shot from a circus cannon, and sailed over the fence into the gathering darkness.

"My goodness," Lura said.

Agnes was stunned. In the empty space where a few seconds ago Bob had been pure energy in motion, had sped like a comet in his orbit, everything was still.

"Are you going to go get him?" Lura said.

After a moment Agnes said, "I imagine so," thinking, Now why did he have to go and do that, but not really feeling all that disturbed, as if nothing could very much disturb her peace.

"You want me to drive you?"

"No," Agnes said. "He won't go far."

"It's getting dark."

"I can see in the dark as well as anyone."

"Well, I didn't mean anything. I just thought I'd offer to help."

"Go on home and get some rest, Lura. You've been through enough for one day."

She left Lura in the yard and went inside to pull on a pair of slacks and a blouse. She hesitated, then from the kitchen beside the refrigerator she got the nightstick Pops always used to carry in his car. She tapped it into her palm. "Damn old dog," she said.

She walked all the way down the street to the thoroughfare, calling, then crossed and turned into an older neighborhood with houses hidden in big heavy-limbed trees. The sidewalk was made of old buckled bricks. Dead downtown was a few blocks away, the air above it all blue and foggy with streetlamp glow. It looked underwater. She picked her way along the uneven brick path, the dry sound of roaches scurrying away from her flip-flops.

The old trees towering over her head were so thick with leaves they were spooky. Agnes harked back to fairy tales heard in her childhood and imagined that she was a child walking in a forest where someone had long ago cut the narrow rumbly streets along old trails.

Big roots hunched up through the crumbly pavement, and here and there a cozy house was nestled deep in amongst the trees like a forest cottage.

She and Pops were married forty-nine years. Sometimes it seemed like the whole thing actually took place, and then sometimes it didn't, as if there was a big blank between when she was a little girl and now. She was only twenty-one when they married. She remembered their honeymoon at the Grand Hotel in Point Clear. They'd walked those old paths draped with that moss like damp shadowy lace. In the room their love was quick and startling, their bodies drawn into it like a child's arm drawn briefly into a hard and painful little muscle.

Agnes slowed her steps as her heart sped up. She remembered kissing Pops in the late years and how it was just pinched-up lips and a dry peck, and remembered kissing him like that in his box, how his lips were like wood and how horrified she'd been. She'd had that craving for a child, briefly, a little bit late, and had not pressed it with Pops. He'd not had word one on the subject. He seemed at times such a passive man, and then at others all pent up. If he'd had passions, she suspected he disapproved of their expression. Perhaps he told them to Bob in the intimacy between a man and his dog, who knows what a man told his dog? He'd always had Bob. There were two other dogs before him, but they were the same kind of dog, looked exactly the same. Every one named Bob. She wondered if he'd have done the same with her if she'd died, just gone out and got another Agnes. If there hadn't been Bob, maybe he'd have talked to her.

Seemed like they had the same dog for forty-nine years. One would die, Pops would get another one just like it the next day. Seemed to have the same obnoxious personality. She'd sometimes catch herself looking at that dog, or one of them, and thinking, This is the longest-living dog I ever saw. She laughed out loud.

She rounded a corner and looked down a narrow street lighted dimly by the old streetlamps. Far down, a little dog stood still in the middle of the road. From what Agnes could make out, it looked like Bob. He seemed to be looking back at her.

She leaned forward, squinting her good eye.

The dog stood very still, looking at her.

"Bob," Agnes said. Then she called out, "Bob! Come here, boy! Oh Bob!"

She moved a little closer. Bob tensed up, stiffened his legs and his neck. Otherwise, he didn't budge.

Agnes clucked to herself and tapped the nightstick into her palm. "Damn old dog. I ought to let him run off somewhere.

"Go on!" she called to him then. "Go on, if you want to."

Bob took a little straightening step. He lifted his head and sniffed the breeze. He was poised there, under the streetlamp, looking proud and aloof, seeming in that foggy distance like the ghost of all the Bobs. She imagined that after fifty years he was asking himself if he wanted any more. Well, she thought, she wouldn't press it: she would let him go where he wanted to go.

She heard a car and looked around. There at the stop sign sat Lura's Impala, like some big pale fish paused on the ocean floor, the headlights its soft glowing eyes seeking. It nosed around the corner headed her way. At that Bob turned and trotted away. She watched him fade into the foggy gloom, just the hint of a sidling slip in his gait. Go on and look around then, she said to herself. Go see what you've been sniffing in the breeze. She couldn't see him then, his image snuffed in the fog.

She stood in the middle of the old quiet street and waited on Lura to pull up. On a lark she turned sideways and stuck out her thumb. The car eased up beside her. She opened the creaky old door and looked in. Lura appeared to be dressed for traveling.

"I got an idea," Agnes said.

At Lura's pace they reached the coast about dawn. They took the long winding road out to the fort, hung a left at the guardhouse, and went down to the beach. Lura, woozy with fatigue, rolled on off the blacktop and into the sand for several yards before the Impala bogged down. She took the gearshift in one white-gloved hand and pushed it up into Park, pushed the headlights knob to the dash, and shut off the engine. Gulls and wader birds called across the marsh. The sky was lightening into blue. Frogs and more birds began to call, and redwings clung to stalks of swaying sea oats.

"Listen to the morning," Lura said.

And Agnes closed both eyes to sleep as the molten sun boiled up, cyclopic, from the water.

A BLESSING

THAT AFTERNOON HER HUSBAND DROVE THEM OUT the old Birmingham highway in the wagon, a 1985 Ford LTD Country Squire he'd bought on a lark in these, the latter days of what she called her great gestation. It was a big, safe car. He drove slowly as always, taking it easy, never straining the wagon's enormous transmission. The car sailed over humps in the road like a yacht over swells in the ocean, and plowed into low-lying dips with a grave and leveling balanced distribution of load.

They sat on the broad front seat as small as children, as if their feet weren't actually touching the floor. The car's long, broad interior even made *her* feel small, with her swollen middle and engorged, stretch-marked, leaky sacs—once girlish breasts she could cup in her palms. Sitting there, she felt like a penitent, pregnant twelve-year-old on an outing with her dad.

After a few miles her husband eased on the wagon's left blinker, looked in the rearview mirror, checked once over his left shoulder, and turned, releasing a convoy of impatient vehicles gathered behind him. In her visor's vanity mirror she caught flashes of the angry faces of drivers who watched the Ford mosey off down the little blacktop road.

It was getting toward late afternoon, the sun dropping in the sky and yellowing in the haze. On the left appeared a lush, rolling pasture where two piebald horses grazed in the shade of a grove and flicked their tails at horseflies.

"Oh, look," she said. "Pintos. Let's stop, just for a minute." She'd ridden horses as a girl, and hoped she would again someday, with their child. Her husband eased the wagon onto the shoulder and came around to help her get out. He held her by the arm while she steadied her legs and rolled her weight from the ball of one swollen foot to another, over to the barbed-wire fence. The wire was rusty. They didn't touch it or try to cross it into the pasture. He whistled a couple of times for the ponies, who looked up from grazing to gaze at them briefly. The smaller one toggled its ears in their direction, and then both bent back down to the sweet-looking grass.

"I wish we had an apple or something," she said.

"We'd better get on," he said. "We'll be late."

She lingered a moment. "It's a good omen," she said, "seeing the ponies."

Omens weren't as important to him as to her, she knew, but he was not unaffected by them. Once, after a breakup, she saw an early star right next to the moon, which was full and distinct as a white communion wafer she might reach up, take, and place upon her tongue. She hadn't taken communion since she was a girl. It had been a very good sign.

He helped her back to the car, and they drove on down the road to a T intersection, where he turned right onto a bumpy lane pocked with potholes and ragged on the edges, as if it had been ripped from the middle of a better road and patched with surplus asphalt. The car jolted and rattled over a washed-out stretch. He slowed even more and looked over at her. She put both hands on her middle as if to steady it.

"I'm okay," she said, patting herself. "Good shocks."

They descended into a wooded ravine and crossed a small bridge over a creek. The water rushed beneath them over what looked like slate and plunged into a lower cut off to their left, disappearing into the thick, intertwined foliage of the woods. She wondered at what sort of wildlife crept in there, what strange small animals. Manimals, she'd called animals when she was a toddler. She'd had a sonogram a couple of months back, and was awed and a little frightened by the baby's alien image on the screen, its wide dark eye sockets and oddly reptilian attitude in the womb. In some ways it was like the grainy, negative image of a nightmare, and yet she felt a profound and overwhelming love the moment she saw it. She was superstitious, she knew, because she had a vulnerable imagination.

The car rose, like an airliner groaning into flight, up the steep other side of the ravine. At the top of the hill he turned right again, onto a hard-packed dirt-and-gravel road that wound into the woods, climbed, and ended in a clearing on top of a knoll from which two narrow drives dropped away.

"I think we take the left one here," her husband said. The drive he indicated, half the width of the dirt-and-gravel road, seemed to lead off into the air at the treetop level of broadleafs that grew down in the canyon. He eased the wagon up to the edge and they peered over it, where they saw a steep and rutted drive that curved sharply at the bottom into a clearing. Through the trees they could see part of a house and beyond that the slanting late-afternoon light glinting on water.

"There must be lakes all through these old canyons," he said. "I wouldn't mind living out here."

The wagon's engine idled alternately high and low, adjusting to the condenser cycling on and off. He turned off the air and rolled down every window in the car, using the control panel on his armrest, then turned off the car. The engine ticked like a conductor's baton upon the music stand, the silence of the woods settled into their ears, and they began to hear the desultory drone of insects, the oddly loud, staccato songs of birds, and some low sound they couldn't distinguish: water, a breeze in the trees, or both.

"It's so quiet."

"I could get used to it," he said.

"Be careful with this dog, okay?"

"I will. I won't get out if it doesn't look right."

"Okay," she said.

"We don't have to get another dog right now, if you don't want to. It's not really important."

"No, it's all right. I know you miss Rowdy."

"Yeah," he said. "I miss him."

"I just want to make sure this dog's—I don't know—good-natured."

"He's got a hard act to follow."

"I know. Rowdy was the best."

"Yep," he said. "He was."

They peered again over the edge of the drive. The car was perched just there.

"Well," he said, "we'd better get on."

He didn't crank the car again, but merely turned the ignition switch to On, dropped the gearshift to Neutral, and allowed the wagon to roll slowly off the knoll and down the narrow drive. It was steep and rutted with erosion, most of its gravel had washed away. The experience was like a slow-motion bronco ride. They were pressed forward into their seat belts and shoulder straps so that her arms actually hung forward toward the dash. She felt a faint, quick wave of nausea and almost wished she hadn't come along.

At the bottom of the hill they turned into a muddy clearing in front of a small brick home and immediately were rushed by three friendly, barking, tail-wagging dogs. As he got out of the car, the dogs mobbed him, rising on their hind legs and raking his clothes with muddy paws, licking his hands. The dogs were so absurdly happy that she couldn't suppress a rush of pleasure at seeing them. They wagged their whole rears, spines curling, tails whipping, and ran back and forth between her open window and her husband, desperate for both their attentions at once, transported into happy madness at their arrival. He looked back at her, delighted, and she laughed out loud.

"What great dogs," she called out the window. Her husband was smiling, tussling with two of the dogs, a big thick-coated shepherd-husky mix with a massive head, and a medium-sized shorthaired dog with white and brown splotches like birthmarks: a plain mutt. The two dogs nipped at his hands and his wrists and pants cuffs. A smaller dog, like a Welsh corgi but surely some mongrel collie mix, wriggled around them, vying for space.

She felt it was safe to get out of the car, so she opened the door and, by rocking backwards a little bit first, rolled out onto her feet. The dogs rushed her but held back, as if sensing she required gentler handling. They brushed and bumped their shoulders and rumps against her, twining themselves around her knees and through her legs, whining in barely suppressed fits of joy. She reached down to scratch the little collie's head and the dog went still, its soft brown eyes looking up into hers. A sudden heaviness in her chest almost brought tears to her eyes.

She knew what this was about, understood mood swings, irrational fears, hormonal problems. She was even brighter probably than her husband, who had earned his Ph.D. but kept his job teaching high school chemistry because he believed it was where he was most needed. She watched him tussle with the dogs, who'd trotted back over to him. She would have become a teacher, too, but for her somewhat fragile self-esteem, which combined with stage fright and sullen students to make the task impossible. Such failure made her angry and impatient with herself. She did not want to seem weak. In regular jobs she was disillusioned by the cynicism people used to survive; they wielded it like medieval broadswords, without grace and with callous indifference to what incidental damage might be done. The small, still dog whose soft coat she stroked with her palm was innocent of all that.

The other two dogs had come back to her, crowding out the smaller dog, and she knelt with determination into the chaos of whipping tails and thrusting snouts, braved the wet swipe of broad pink tongues across her face. She saw her husband straighten up and face the house, brushing his hands off on his khaki trousers as a short, thick man walked around the corner and approached them. He wore a neat flannel shirt, jeans, and a pair of knee-high white rubber boots over the jeans leggings. His broad square face was clean-shaven and his hair was cut in a careless, outgrown flattop. She guessed his age at about fifty. The butt of a small pistol protruded from a short leather holster on his belt.

"Hello," her husband said. "We called about buying a dog?"

The man nodded.

"Which one you want?"

Her husband paused, then looked at her.

"Well," he said, looking at the dogs, who were wriggling and trotting back and forth between them and the man. The man paid the dogs no attention. "I spoke to someone—your wife?—and I think she said you had a young retriever mix. A golden."

The man pointed briefly at the big dog.

"How about him?"

Her husband reached down to stroke the shepherd-husky's head, and then looked at his wife where she knelt carefully, allowing the little collie and the brown-and-white dog to nuzzle her. She glanced at the house and saw that shades were drawn over the windows. Where there'd once been shrubs around the house were bare brown stalks, the gray earth around them worn and pocked with smooth depressions where she guessed the dogs lay cooling during the day. The screened door of a back porch hung open, its wire sections browned and splayed from their frames. She put her hands on her knees and pushed herself to her feet.

"Is the retriever around?" she said.

"Well, the retriever," the man said, "I sold him."

"That's too bad," her husband said after a moment. "When we spoke to your wife this morning she said we could come and get the retriever this afternoon."

"Well," the man said, reaching down to pick up a small fallen branch and toss it into the brush at the edge of the yard, "she don't know what's here and what ain't. I had to get rid of that dog. He give me some trouble this morning."

Her husband became somber and closed. He fixed

his eyes on the other man, who then looked up and regarded them with disdain, it seemed: first her husband, and then her. It alarmed her to be looked at so directly. His eyes held no trace of compassion. He cared no more for them than he did for these dogs.

"All right, then," her husband said. "You want to sell us one of these dogs?"

"No," the man said. "Just take whichever one you want."

"You're giving them away?"

"That's right."

"We'd be glad to pay. I understood from your wife they've had their shots."

The man seemed distracted. He hawked and spat an amoeboid glob onto the dirt.

"It really don't make any difference to me," he said. "These strays come up out the woods. She can't stand their barking and carrying on. Take them all if you want to. Put them in that big station wagon and take them off." He squared off and looked each of them in each face. "I don't give a tinker's damn. It wadn't my ad in the paper."

She saw her husband's face slowly darken with anger. He pushed his hands into his pants pockets and she saw his lips tighten.

After a moment he said, "I can see there's been a misunderstanding. I think we'll just call it off."

"Suit yourself," said the man. He went back around the corner of the house. The big dog followed him, then in a second came trotting back to them.

Her husband had stood there a moment, looking at

the ground, his face clenched, both fists jammed into his pockets. "We ought to take them all, that son of a bitch," he said. He kneeled to pet the dogs again and they leapt to him, each desperately trying to get all of his attention. The little collie, squeezed out, began to growl. It tried to work its head in between the big dog and the brown-and-white dog and, when they wouldn't let it, snarled and lunged for the brown-and-white dog's throat.

"Oh my God," she said.

Her husband jumped back and stood up. The collie growled and hung on to the brown-and-white dog's throat, and the brown-and-white dog tried to get away by holding its head up and hopping backwards. But the little collie, pulled up onto its hind legs with the other dog's hopping, held on tight. The brown-and-white dog began to cry in high, piercing yelps.

"Stop it," the woman shouted at them. Her husband shouted, "Hey!" and clapped his hands. But the dogs, their wild eyes inches apart, ignored them.

The big dog, the shepherd-husky mix, tried to shoulder the collie away from the brown-and-white dog, failed, and then trotted happily over to her husband again, tail wagging.

The brown-and-white dog had lowered its neck to the ground and tried to roll over in submission, but the little collie, instead of letting go, yanked hard, and the brown-and-white dog hollered, loudly this time, and got back to its feet.

The owner came walking back around the corner from behind the house.

"She just attacked him," the woman said.

The man reached down and grabbed the collie by the nape of the neck and pulled, but it hung on to the brown-and-white dog, who hollered even louder, yelping in pain. She could see small grooves of pink flesh where the collie's teeth had torn the brown-and-white dog's skin.

"She's hurting him," she said.

The man finally spoke.

"Goddamn you little bitch," he said to the little dog.

"Can I help?" her husband said. "Where's your water hose?" He stood a few feet apart from the dogs and the man, his arms helplessly at his sides.

The man reached to his waist and drew the small pistol and put it to the little dog's head.

"No!" she said. The man looked at her.

"Jesus," her husband said.

"You want her to kill him?" the man said to her. "Which one you want to die?"

She was in tears.

"Just make them stop," she said.

"Get those dogs away from my wife," her husband said, his voice strange with emotion. "Don't shoot that gun. Get those dogs out of here."

The man turned to her husband and said, "Just where the hell do you think you are?"

They stared at one another and she felt her heart seize down in her chest.

"No," she said, almost to herself.

The two dogs, their eyes rolled back, were frozen in their struggle, the little dog's teeth locked onto the other dog's neck. For a moment, no one moved. The big dog, the shepherd-husky mix, paced nervously among them.

The man shoved the pistol back into its holster and grabbed both dogs by the loose skin behind their necks. He lifted them into the air and carried them, still attached teeth-to-throat, the brown-and-white dog crying the whole way, around back of the house to the lake. The woman and her husband followed partway and stopped as the man waded into the lake carrying the two dogs and then plunged them both into the water. When he brought them up again, the little dog had let go.

"Thank God," she whispered. Her mouth and throat had gone dry with fear.

The brown-and-white dog paddled to shore and shook himself hard, the droplets clear and distinct as tiny glass beads in the slanting afternoon sunlight. He trotted away down the bank. The man waded out deeper with the collie, put both hands around her neck, shoved her under the water, and held her there.

Even from where they stood she could see him struggling to hold her under. His shirt was wet, and she could see the muscles on his thick shoulders bunch together with the strain. She could see air bubbles break the surface above where he held her. She could see the man's neck turn a deep red.

She tried to speak but couldn't. The muscles in her throat wouldn't respond. She wanted to call out and claim the little dog, try to save her life, but she couldn't move.

It took a long time. The late sunlight broke through the trees on the high ridge across the lake as if through a prism. The moment was incomprehensibly beautiful, full of grief. She felt the knotted fear in her heart dissolve, and a strange and deeply seated sense of loss washed through her. She wept in broken, childlike sobs and held her husband tight, his frame bent over her middle as if for protection, his lips next to her ear quietly saying shh, shh, shh, but she was lost in this. When she was done they were alone, the water's surface undisturbed, and the sun gone down behind the high ridge across the lake.

Together they walked back to the car. He opened her door and helped her get in. They eased back up the steep and rutted drive without speaking. At the top of the hill, the brown-and-white dog and the shepherd-husky plunged from the woods and ran alongside the car down the dirt road, silent, and then dropped back, and stood in the road with their tongues out, watching them go.

When the car turned onto the blacktop road again the low sun's light shot through gaps in the trees and hit the windshield straight-on, exploding. The glare was like a blow to her eyes. Her husband held his hand out before him and slowed the car to a crawl. She'd thrown up her own hands instinctively, but now she lowered them and held her eyes open. She saw a hot white hole burn into the air, the world around it black as smoldering paper. She felt the light go into her brain. She felt it move down through her and into her child, like the infusion of knowledge.

A RETREAT

I HAD MY GEAR ALL PACKED WHEN IVAN KNOCKED. A group of us was going down to his family's farm on the Louisiana line. He came in, wearing his down vest and hunting boots, smoking a Marlboro in the side of his mouth, one eye squinted against the smoke.

"Ready?" he said.

"Yeah. Who's riding with us?"

"Just you and me, in the pickup."

I thought maybe the others had already gone on down in Ivan and MaeRose's Caddy, a 1972 Seville, powder blue. I looked at him and he shrugged.

"What?" I said.

So then he told me, blurting it out in about two sentences, this huge story: He and Eve had been having an affair, she told Dave about it last night, and Dave called up MaeRose and told her.

Jesus Christ.

"It's been going on awhile, she couldn't stand it anymore," Ivan said. He looked at me, then looked away. "Look, I'll make a confession. We've been meeting each other here in your place the last couple of months. I don't know, maybe longer."

"Here?" I couldn't believe it. I'd loaned Ivan a key so he could use my computer while I was at school. Or so he'd said.

"In my bed?" I said.

"In the bed, yeah." He patted the sofa cushion. "On the couch. On the floor, on that rug there. Out on the screened porch. In the car, one day, down by the bamboo, when you were home."

I went to the window and looked down there.

"I didn't see you."

Ivan stood up and went into the bathroom, dropped his cigarette into the toilet, took a piss, flushed. He came back out and sat down on the sofa. "The fact is, I'm going to need a place to stay for a while. MaeRose asked me not to come back until she leaves. She's gonna stay with her parents for a while."

"Will you try to work it out?"

He shook his head, looked at his watch.

"She's filing for divorce right about now, I imagine." He lit another cigarette. "You know, she hasn't been exactly immaculate, herself."

I didn't know anything about it. Ivan got up to go into the kitchen. He rummaged in the cabinet for the bourbon, found my bottle of Ezra, pulled the cork and took a swig, corked it, and put it back into the cabinet. He came back into the living room. He was looking around at the walls, as if there was something missing, a painting or a window or something.

"So, you still want to go?" he said. "I'm going. I got to get away until this all calms down a little bit."

I stood in the living room trying to comprehend it all. You think you know what's going on around you, what your friends are up to, and then they turn out to have these secret lives. I couldn't believe he and Eve had been fucking in my bed. When was the last time I'd gotten laid in that bed? As a matter of fact, I myself had fantasized about Eve in that bed, because she'd flirted with me at a party. In fact, she'd flirted with me in front of Dave, and I'd wondered what the hell she was up to. Another time, during a party at their house, Eve and I had been in her study, talking. Dave opened the side door, from the bathroom, stuck his head in, glared at us, then pulled his head out and slammed the door. So, yeah, I knew something was going on, but I didn't know what. I wondered what the hell she was up to.

Fucking Ivan the whole time. I was a little depressed by the news. I'd been depressed in general for something like five or six years. This little setback, of course, was different. Nothing like the real thing. But it all adds up. I'd gone back to school, and I was hanging in there but not too well. I hadn't gone in with a plan. I'd tried moving in with a buddy of mine and that didn't work, I couldn't suppress my desire to hole up, hide. I'd moved into this apartment when the old fellow living here died, he'd been holed up chain-smoking in it for twenty years. He was a retired professor of mathematics, a recluse who'd scrawled his last message on a scrap of notebook paper in shaky pencil: "Gone out—be back in a few minutes." And then he didn't go out, he took an overdose of pills and went to bed and died. A friend of mine who lived across the hall from him, in the habit of checking on him, found his body and called the police. She was shaken as she showed me around the next day. We found his note and a large half-empty bottle of phenobarbital. One thin dark suit clung to a closet hanger as if to a frame of old bones. Nothing at all in the chest of drawers. Not a morsel of food in the apartment. No roaches. No reason for them to hang around. He lived off cigarettes and coffee and barbiturates.

I moved in and scrubbed streaks of tobacco smoke residue off all the woodwork with Formula 409. The stove was dusty but otherwise clean. The refrigerator was empty except for a two-month-old carton of half-and-half stuck to the shelf. I stripped up the old stained indoor-outdoor carpet from the floors and sanded the wood down to reveal a beautiful blond oak. I rubbed in Johnson's Wax with my hands, buffed it with a rented machine, and then I lay out in the middle of the empty, polished expanse of narrow oak boards, my eye to the floor, each board like a golden lane leaping up and away down a gleaming runway. I marveled at the almost tactile sense of starting over, the clarity of vision, the simplicity and beauty of the big open room. From where I lay, the windows looked out upon open sky, a great big protective bubble of opportunity. I'd gone back to school to make something of my life, I could do anything in the world. I'd concentrate and get it done. But within two weeks all the bad stuff had seeped back in. The staying home and skipping classes, the looking out windows at people in cars at the stoplight, at people walking by on the sidewalk, at people on the sidewalk stopped to talk, at people who glanced up and saw me watching them, spoke to one another, and then looked up as I stood there looking back. Strangers.

I figured the old professor probably had a pretty good life when he was about my age, and this unnerved me. I wished I'd kept his phenobarbital, just to keep myself calm. I've never had the slightest leaning toward suicide. I always think if I can wait it out, things will change. I wondered how long the old professor had felt that way.

"What about it, Jack?" Ivan said. "We going?"

I thought about it, and said, "Sure."

"Don't get so excited," he said.

"I was just thinking about things."

"You're in no shape to do that," he said. I had to laugh, a little anyway. I picked up my bags and we went downstairs. It was one of those cold and windy, drizzly days and we hurried across the yard. Ivan's truck had a camper shell over the bed, and I tossed my stuff in there next to his young retriever, Mary, who stood there with her head ducked, wagging her tail. There were sliding windows from there to the cab, and Mary stuck her head through and let her tongue drip onto the seat between us as we got settled and strapped on the seat belts.

I said, "So you get Mary?"

"Sure," Ivan said. "That's an old trick. They leave you with all the stuff, even the animals, and you can't get rid of them or don't want to, and you've got all this shit reminding you of how you fucked up, and these dogs or cats or squawking parakeets or whatever reminding you of everything you did together, and so when they've gone they've cut themselves completely loose, no strings, clean slate. You've got all the baggage. Next time you see them, they've lost weight and cut their hair and feel just great about themselves, got their teeth cleaned, stopped biting their nails. They've got the soul of a bluebird. You realize they were absolutely miserable with you all along."

Ivan passed me a little skinny he'd rolled up earlier. I lit it, poured myself a cup of coffee from his heavy green thermos, and we pulled out, rolling past the thick stand of bamboo that rose up tall beside the old Victorian apartment house, the sharp-leaved tops tossing in the wind. They were as tall as the eaves and their leaves brushed against my screened porch. The blackbirds and grackles that had ventured from that protective thicket were already returning in little squadrons of threes and fours. As we turned onto the boulevard to the highway, I rolled down my window and let out a whoop, just like a kid. Ivan looked at me and laughed. We knew this retreat would be a success.

WE WERE STILL UNDER THE COLD AND MISTY FRONT WHEN we crossed the cattle guard into the farm, and we unloaded our gear in a hurry and took it into the farmhouse and built a fire to take the chill out of the room. I put my hands on the old plaster walls. They were as cold as the truck's windows had been out on the road.

In a little while, the great room felt drier and warmer. We had a cup of thick chicory coffee and stood in front of the fire, then pulled on our jackets and boots and got the guns, coaxed young Mary away from the rug in front of the fire—she didn't want to get up, kept her chin flat on the rug with her big brown eyes looking up at us, hoping we'd leave her alone—and headed out to walk the fenceline.

There's something fine about walking a fenceline through wet fields in a steady, misting rain when you're all wrapped up against it. The world is reaching saturation, the air is uniformly cool and wet. It wraps around you like your heavy clothing and feels close and somehow invigorating. I don't know. I guess it has the opposite effect on some people, but it strikes a chord in me. You slop through the muddy fields and get a little numb with it and something inside of you lets go a little bit. There's nothing else like it. Walking in the cold and dry is fine, too, but it's not the same thing. Walking in the rain loosens up the bad things inside. You feel good, your heart is big enough for any sorrow. You're walking, slogging, and you're feeling strong. The dog's trotting here and there, aimless, nosing around, stumbling onto wet coveys and then leaping like a fool dog when they burst past her. No one's critical. You take an occasional shot at a bird, bag a couple, just enough to make dinner's rice interesting. No big take. No worry. No desire for more than you need. It's a walk as much as a hunt. We didn't talk about the women. We didn't say anything much.

We walked all over that thousand acres. The trees bordering the far ends of the pastures looked more like the ghosts of trees in the gray mist. We'd bagged a few quail along the fencelines and beside the creek. Way over by the hay rolls on the north rise we flushed some birds that flew into a low, dense grove of miscellaneous hardwoods. We spread out and walked through the grove, taking shots when the birds flushed, one here, two there, missing. There were still leaves, black and wet, along the gnarled branches that twisted from the short, stout trunks. The birds weaved in short bursts of flight, staying just out of range. At the far end of the grove we stopped and had a smoke.

We stood and smoked, not talking, and then Ivan caught my eye and nodded at something on the ground a few feet ahead. It was a rabbit, a young cottontail, sitting as still as could be. But when we saw it, young Mary saw it, and she leapt.

The rabbit dashed from the edge of the grove and into the adjoining pasture. Instinctively we shot, hobbling it just as it topped a little hummock, and then Mary zoomed over after it and disappeared. We heard a small, high scream, and then a crunching sound that carried with remarkable clarity in the wet, chilly air. It was an awful sound. Mary came trotting back up over the hummock with the rabbit hanging limp by its head from her jaws. She stepped back through the fence, sat down in the grass a few feet away from us, and started licking the rabbit's fur.

"Christ," Ivan said. "It's just a little thing. It's not even a rabbit. It's a *bunny.*"

I felt pretty bad about shooting it, too. Mary had

begun to toss the rabbit up into the air. Ivan shook his head.

"Hey," he said to Mary. "Hey!" He took the rabbit from her and she leapt up into the air after it, playing.

"Leave it," Ivan said. "Sit." She looked at him, cocked her head. "Sit!" She sat and looked away, out into the field where she'd caught up with the rabbit.

Ivan put the rabbit into his jacket's pouch, and we walked back to the house, Mary sniffing at Ivan's jacket and pawing at the backs of his legs. We flushed a few birds on the way but didn't take a shot. When we reached the house we followed the gravel drive around back and walked to the bridge over the creek. We took out the five birds and the rabbit and set them on the bridge timbers next to the railing, blocking Mary out with our arms. She stuffed her snout beneath Ivan's armpit and stayed there for a moment, her nostrils working.

"What are we going to do with the rabbit?" I said.

"I guess we'll clean it," Ivan said. "We may as well eat it. We might as well eat our little rabbit brother."

"I don't really want to clean it," I said.

Ivan gave me the birds and said he'd clean the rabbit. As I cleaned the birds I dropped the feathers and entrails and the heads into the creek and watched them float downstream. Ivan dumped the rabbit's viscera into the stream, too, so Mary wouldn't get into it. He tacked the skin high on a broken branch, and Mary sat beneath it looking up, not knowing whether to jump at it or not. She rose and sat and rose and sat, restlessly. Ivan came up behind me and stuck something into my back pocket. It was one of the rabbit's feet. I pulled it out and looked.

"Pretty grisly," I said.

"Unlucky rabbit," Ivan said. "He takes on all your bad luck for you now."

"Okay." I tucked the foot into the fob pocket of my jeans.

We went in and pulled off our boots, stoked the coals in the hearth and added wood, and poured a little whiskey while we sat in front of the fire drying our socks and pants leggings. We had a couple of stiff bourbons. Then we went into the kitchen to put together a meal. Ivan took the rabbit out of the refrigerator and we looked at it. Maybe it was the old anatomy charts in school that showed the muscle, the elliptical bands of sinew overlapping one other, symmetrically joined. I couldn't stand to look at it.

"It looks human," I said.

Ivan looked at me, then set the rabbit on the counter and studied it.

"Christ," he said. "You fucker. Enough about the rabbit."

He laughed. We both laughed so hard we had to set our drinks down and lean against the counter and wheeze it off.

"I don't know how to cook it," he said. "Let's just put it on the fire. There's a spit in there."

He took the rabbit into the living room and pushed the spit through it and placed the ends of the spit into the cradles. I went back into the kitchen to whip up something for the quail. I don't have the same kind of problem with birds. It's all those grocery store fryers, I guess. Conditioning. I wrapped the quail in bacon and set them in a dish of rice and mushrooms and chopped green onions and slid them into the oven, and dropped some fresh green beans into the steamer. I'd come back in and turn them on last.

We sipped the whiskey and dried our socks and every few minutes one of us got up to turn the rabbit. After a while it began to lighten and then to brown. Mary lay on the carpet and watched it with us.

Pretty soon I was more relaxed than I had been in over a year. Outside the tall windows that looked out back in the dusk, great flocks of birds flowed in a fluctuating stream across the sky. I thought of how the redwing blackbirds and grackles gathered mornings and evenings in the bamboo thicket outside my screened porch. I have sat there and watched them, as evening ticked down, swoop in twos, threes, fours, and disappear into the bamboo until the whole thicket was alive with birds hidden by the bamboo leaves, invisible birds, the noise like a thousand old doors swinging on rusty, creaking hinges. In the mornings as they wake they take it up again, and burst from the thicket in bunches. It makes for some pretty strange dreams.

Sometimes in the dawn hour, the birds get so loud they wake me up and I lie there surrounded by their weird cacophonous voices, thinking about the Great Fuckup, and imagining all their beady little eyes darting around in that jungle green like all my quirky little demons. I'd married so young and didn't know anything about it, and lost my wife and baby son when I was twenty-one years old, let them go with a kind of despair I could not begin to even recognize. It was true I didn't love her at all. But it was just like Ivan had joked as we'd left that morning: she left the furniture, the silverware, the pots and pans, the television, the books, the carpet, the food, the car, her prescription medicines, her shower cap, shampoo, toothbrush, hairbrush, stuffed animals collection, inessential clothing, old letters and postcards, sheets and towels, cheap framed prints on the walls, stereo, and all the photo albums except the one devoted to our little boy. And she took him. And over the next few years things had shut down inside me with the regularity of lights in an empty warehouse where a night watchman is pulling the switches one by one. I moved around, went back to school, moved in with a friend and then moved out again, into the old man's empty apartment. And finally one morning that spring I lay there awake, the small bedroom full of the blackbirds' strange and beautifully dissonant warbling, and couldn't think of what I really cared about anymore.

I said to Ivan, "Did you ever fuck Eve while those blackbirds were all out there in the bamboo?"

He poked at the fire a minute.

"What, when they're all out there raising hell? It's like fucking in the middle of a goddamn asylum," he said. "You don't know where you are when it's over."

I said, "In my bed."

He laughed.

I said, "What are y'all going to do?"

He didn't say anything, and tossed another split log onto the fire.

"I don't know," he said then. "It's not going to be much fun for a while."

"I don't think I could ever do it again," I said. "Go through a divorce. I don't think I'd ever divorce again, at least not with children."

"Then don't remarry," Ivan said.

"At least you don't have children."

We left the rabbit over the coals while we ate the quail, rice, and green beans. It was quiet in the room and warm. Ivan held up a glass of wine. I held mine up.

"Well," he said, "fuck all of them, Jack. You know?"

"Fuck them each and every one," I said, and had to shut my mouth and look away. I got up and went into the living room to the fire, put oven mittens on my hands, and lifted the spit with the rabbit out of its cradles. That took a little while. I carried it back into the dining room and laid it across the plate with the birds. Cooked, the rabbit wasn't as disturbing to me. But the meat was tough and gamy.

"Should've at least put a little butter and salt and pepper on it," Ivan said.

"I wish we hadn't shot it," I said.

"Enough about that!" Ivan said. "We'll give it to Mary."

"That's a good idea."

"Mary killed it. She finished it off."

"In innocence."

"Exactly. It's Mary's rabbit."

"Okay."

We gave it to Mary. She trotted back into the living

room and lay down in front of the fire with the rabbit under her front paws and began to eat it almost delicately, sniffing it and licking it as if it were her pup and she were eating it almost lovingly in maternal wonder. But when she began to crunch on the bones we sent her outside.

WE GOT UP LATE, WALKED THE FIELDS THE NEXT DAY. ON the evening before we left I went out by myself to walk the fencelines in the fields behind the house. Dusk settled in. I had the little rabbit's foot in my pocket. The drizzling rain had stopped and things were very quiet. I walked down a narrow corridor made by a row of young pines set out from the edge of a thicket. I could hardly see, with dark advancing, but I spooked a single dove from one of the pines and as he flew away down the corridor against the darkening sky, I took a shot. It must have been low, confusing him, because he turned in a sort of abrupt Immelmann and headed straight back down the corridor at me. I leveled the gun and shot, but missed again—I forgot to aim high—and he darted out of the corridor and across the field.

I could hear the last shot echo over field after field, and then a great silence. A strange ecstasy sang in my veins like a drug. I raised the gun and fired the last shell into the air, the flame from the barrel against the darkening sky, and the chamber locked open, empty. Then silence. Not even a sifting of wind in the leaves. Not a single wheezy note from a blackbird, or any other kind of bird. I wanted the moment to last forever.

BILL

WILHELMINA, EIGHTY-SEVEN, LIVED ALONE IN THE same town as her two children, but she rarely saw them. Her main companion was a trembling poodle she'd had for about fifteen years, named Bill. You never hear of dogs named Bill. Her husband in his decline had bought him, named him after a boy he'd known in the Great War, and then wouldn't have anything to do with him. He'd always been Wilhelmina's dog. She could talk to Bill in a way that she couldn't talk to anyone else, not even her own children.

Not even her husband, now nearly a vegetable out at King's Daughters' Rest Home on the old highway.

She rose in the blue candlelight morning to go see him about the dog, who was doing poorly. She was afraid of being completely alone.

There were her children and their children, and

even some great-grandchildren, but that was neither here nor there for Wilhelmina. They were all in different worlds.

She drove her immaculate ocean-blue Delta 88 out to the home and turned up the long, barren drive. The tall naked trunks of a few old pines lined the way, their sparse tops distant as clouds. Wilhelmina pulled into the parking lot and took two spaces so she'd have plenty of room to back out when she left. She paused for a moment to check herself in the rearview mirror, and adjusted the broad-brimmed hat she wore to hide the thinning spot on top of her head.

Her husband, Howard, lay propped up and twisted in his old velour robe, his mouth open, watching TV. His thick white hair stood in a matted knot on his head like a child's.

"What?" he said when she walked in. "What did you say?"

"I said, 'Hello!' Wilhelmina replied, though she'd said nothing.

She sat down.

"I came to tell you about Bill, Howard. He's almost completely blind now and he can't go to the bathroom properly. The veterinarian says he's in pain and he's not going to get better and I should put him to sleep."

Her husband had tears in his eyes.

"Poor old Bill," he said.

"I know," Wilhelmina said, welling up herself now. "I'll miss him so."

"I loved him at Belleau Wood! He was all bloody and walking around," Howard said. "They shot off his nose in the Meuse-Argonne." He picked up the remote box and held the button down, the channels thumping past like the muted thud of an ancient machine gun.

Wilhelmina dried her tears with a Kleenex from her handbag and looked up at him.

"Oh, fiddle," she said.

"Breakfast time," said an attendant, a slim copper-colored man whose blue smock was tailored at the waist and flared over his hips like a suit jacket. He set down the tray and held his long delicate hands before him as if for inspection.

He turned to Wilhelmina.

"Would you like to feed your husband, ma'am?"

"Heavens, no," Wilhelmina said. She shrank back as if he intended to touch her with those hands.

When the attendant held a spoonful of oatmeal up to her husband's mouth he lunged for it, his old gray tongue out, and slurped it down.

"Oh, he's ravenous today," said the attendant. Wilhelmina, horrified, felt for a moment as if she were losing her mind and had wandered into this stranger's room by mistake. She clutched her purse and slipped out into the hall.

"I'm going," she called faintly, and hurried out to her car, which sat on the cracked surface of the parking lot like an old beached yacht. The engine groaned, turned over, and she steered down the long drive and onto the highway without even a glance at the traffic. A car passed her on the right, up in the grass, horn blaring, and an enormous dump truck cleaved the air to her left like a thunderclap. She would pay them no mind.

When she got home the red light on her answering

machine, a gift from her son, was blinking. It was him on the tape.

"I got your message about Bill, Mama. I'll take him to the vet in the morning, if you want. Just give me a call. Bye-bye, now."

"No, I can't think about it," Wilhelmina said.

Bill was on his cedar-filled pillow in the den. He looked around for her, his nose up in the air.

"Over here, Bill," Wilhelmina said loudly for the dog's deaf ears. She carried him a Milk-Bone biscuit, for his teeth were surprisingly good. He sniffed the biscuit, then took it carefully between his teeth, bit off a piece, and chewed.

"Good boy, good Bill."

Bill didn't finish the biscuit. He laid his head down on the cedar pillow and breathed heavily. In a minute he got up and made his halting, wobbling way toward his water bowl in the kitchen, but hit his head on the doorjamb and fell over.

"Oh, Bill, I can't stand it," Wilhelmina said, rushing to him. She stroked his head until he calmed down, and then she dragged him gently to his bowl, where he lapped and lapped until she had to refill it, he drank so much. He kept drinking.

"Kidneys," Wilhelmina said, picking up the bowl. "That's enough, boy."

Bill nosed around for the water bowl, confused. He tried to squat, legs trembling, and began to whine. Wilhelmina carried him out to the backyard, set him down, and massaged his kidneys the way the vet had shown her, and finally a little trickle ran down Bill's left hind leg. He tried to lift it.

"Good old Bill," she said. "You try, don't you?"

She carried him back in and dried his leg with some paper towels.

"I guess I'd do anything for you, Bill," she said. But she had made up her mind. She picked up the phone and called her son. It rang four times and then his wife's voice answered.

"You've reached two-eight-one," she began.

"I know that," Wilhelmina muttered.

". . . We can't come to the phone right now . . ."

Wilhelmina thought that sort of message was rude. If they were there, they could come to the phone.

". . . leave your message after the beep."

"I guess you better come and get Bill in the morning," Wilhelmina said, and hung up.

Wilhelmina's husband had been a butcher, and Katrina, the young widow who'd succeeded him at the market, still brought meat by the house every Saturday afternoon—steaks, roasts, young chickens, stew beef, soup bones, whole hams, bacon, pork chops, ground chuck. Once she even brought a leg of lamb. Wilhelmina couldn't possibly eat it all, so she stored most of it in her deep freeze.

She went out to the porch and gathered as much from the deep freeze as she could carry, dumped it into the kitchen sink like a load of kindling, then pulled her cookbooks from the cupboard and sat down at the kitchen table. She began looking up recipes that had always seemed too complex for her, dishes that sounded vaguely exotic, chose six of the most interesting she could find, and copied them onto a legal pad. Then she made a quick trip to the grocery store to find the items she didn't have on hand, buying odd spices like saffron and coriander, and not just produce but shallots and bright red bell peppers, and a bulb of garlic cloves as big as her fist. Bill had always liked garlic.

Back home, she spread all the meat out on the counter, the chops and steaks and ham, the roast and the bacon, some Italian sausage she'd found, some boudin that had been there for ages, and even a big piece of fish filet. She chopped the sweet peppers, the shallots, ground the spices. The more she worked, the less she thought of the recipes, until she'd become a marvel of culinary innovativeness, combining oils and spices and herbs and meats into the most savory dishes you could imagine: Master William's Sirloin Surprise, Ham au Bill, Bill's Leg of Lamb with Bacon Chestnuts, Bill's Broiled Red Snapper with Butter and Crab, Bloody Boudin à la Bill, and one she decided to call simply Sausage Chops. She fired up her oven, lit every eye on her stove, and cooked it all just as if she were serving the king of France instead of her old French poodle. Then she arranged the dishes on her best china, cut the meat into bite-sized pieces, and served them to her closest friend, her dog.

She began serving early in the evening, letting Bill eat just as much or as little as he wanted from each dish. "This ought to wake up your senses, Bill." Indeed, Bill's interest was piqued. He ate, rested, ate a little more, of this dish and that. He went back to the leg of lamb, nibbling the bacon chestnuts off its sides. Wilhelmina kept gently urging him to eat. And as the evening wore on, Bill's old cataracted eyes gradually seemed to reflect something, it seemed, like quiet suffering—not his usual burden, but the luxurious suffering of the glutton. He had found a strength beyond himself, and so he kept bravely on, forcing himself to eat, until he could not swallow another bite and lay carefully beside the remains of his feast, and slept.

Wilhelmina sat quietly in a kitchen chair and watched from her window as the sun edged up behind the trees, red and molten like the swollen, dying star of an ancient world. She was so tired that her body felt weightless, as if she'd already left it hollow of her spirit. It seemed that she had lived such a long time. Howard had courted her in a horse-drawn wagon. An entire world of souls had disappeared in their time, and other nameless souls had filled their spaces. Some one of them had taken Howard's soul.

Bill had rolled onto his side in sleep, his tongue slack on the floor, his poor stomach as round and taut as a honeydew melon. After such a gorging, there normally would be hell to pay. But Wilhelmina would not allow that to happen.

"I'll take you to the doctor myself, old Bill," she said.

As if in response, a faint and easy dream-howl escaped Bill's throat, someone calling another in the big woods, across empty fields and deep silent stands of trees. *Ooooooo,* it went, high and soft. *Ooooooo.*

Wilhelmina's heart thickened with emotion. Her voice was deep and rich with it.

Hoooooo, she called softly to Bill's sleeping ears.

Oooooo, Bill called again, a little stronger, and she responded, *Hoooooo,* their pure wordless language like echoes in the morning air.

THE WAKE

THE GRIZZLED BITCH LAY ON HER SIDE IN THE FADing sunlight in Sam's front yard, her black wrinkled teats lumped beside her like stillborn pups. It had been a sunny late-October day but now cool evening crept along the edge of the sky and Sam could see the dog's sides shiver as she labored to breathe. Her dark coat was patchy with mange and her eyes looked bad. When Sam walked closer they went to slits and a low growl came from her throat. He could smell her from ten feet away: a ripe, sweet rotten smell. Sam went back inside and called the pound.

When the pound truck cruised slowly by the house at dusk the dog had disappeared. Sam, fresh from the shower and drinking a can of Miller Lite, walked out to the street and told the two men in the truck what the dog looked like. The driver adjusted his cap, spat out the window past Sam, and said likely she went off into the woods to die. He looked at the can of Lite, nodded at Sam, and pulled away. At the spot where the dog had lain in the yard, Sam saw maggots curling and uncurling on the grass.

That night he was awakened by a long yowling moan beneath the floorboards. A latent, heavy loneliness welled in his chest. He went out to the porch. A good breeze had stirred up, and he thought for just a second he could smell the dog. Except for the wind rattling the dry leaves it was quiet.

The next morning, Saturday, Sam went out back with the shovel. There was a big hole in the crawlspace wall near the back door where cats went beneath the house sometimes to have their litters. It somehow made sense a dog would go there to die. Sam started digging.

He heard a truck pull up in front and stuck the shovel into the hard clay of the shallow hole. A UPS man stood in the street behind his van, writing on a clipboard pad, his paper flipping in the wind.

"Sam Beamon?"

Sam nodded. "Something for me?"

"Yes, sir," said the man, a small black fellow whose crewcut head sloped upward toward the crown like a tilted egg. His name tag said "Henry."

"Sign right here on the line, please."

"What is it?"

"Doesn't say."

"You sure it's for me?"

"If you're Sam Beamon."

"Well," Sam said. "What the hell."

Sam signed. Henry hopped up into the truck and grabbed a wooden crate that came up to his belt.

"It's heavy," he said, sliding the crate toward the lift. He hopped down, flipped a chrome toggle switch; there was a high grinding whine and the lift descended with the crate to the street. Sam stepped onto the platform and knocked on the wood.

"I guess I could use this box to bury the dog in, if I wanted to." He looked at Henry. "Seems kind of undignified, to be buried without a box, doesn't it? Uncivilized."

"I don't know," said the man. "For a dog."

"It's not really my dog," Sam said. "But she died here, I think. Under the house."

Henry shrugged and looked at the box, then gazed off at the trees. The breeze gently rattled the leaves.

He heaved at the dolly. Sam directed him up the porch, through the living room, and into a corner of the dining room, which sat between the living room and the kitchen. The house was an old frame home with creaky floors, and the three rooms ran straight back shotgun-fashion, bedrooms off to the right. The kitchen had a door to the backyard.

Sam watched Henry unstrap the dolly and set the crate in the dining room. He wondered if he should have Henry move it to the garage, instead. No way to know, until he knew what it was.

"Where'd this come from?" he said.

Henry checked the ticket.

"New Orleans."

"New Orleans?" Sam said. He looked at the crate again.

Henry said, "You going to open it now?"

Sam looked at him absently.

"Hmm? Oh. I don't know."

They both looked at the box for a moment.

"Well," Henry said. "Got to go." He checked his clipboard again, then wrapped the loose straps around the dolly's frame. He pulled it behind him to the front door and looked back.

"It's an unusual box, you know," he said.

Sam didn't answer, not comprehending.

"Bigger, I mean," Henry said. "Made of wood like that, heavy."

They both looked again at the box.

"Well," Henry said. "Have a nice day." Then he went out, leaving the front door open. Sam heard the dolly rattle down the steps, heard the van door slide shut, then walked out onto the porch and watched him drive away. He went back in and stood beside the crate. He thought he could smell the dog underneath the house, faintly, but then again wasn't sure, thought it could have been his imagination. If he could smell it up here already, it would be bad getting her out of the crawl space. He should be finishing the grave. He had almost decided to do this when the box spoke up.

"Sam?"

He felt his skin go cool.

"Who's there?" he said.

There was laughter from the box.

"Sam," the voice said. "It's me, Marcia."

"Marcia?"

A small plug in the box's side began to wiggle its way out and then dropped to the floor, rolling a few inches to the wall. Sam knelt down warily and brought his eye up to the hole. A brown eye stared back at him. He smelled gardenias. Her perfume. He sat back onto the floor. The sight of her eye, so close, the smell of gardenias. He felt aroused, then ridiculous. Sitting in his dining room with a woman inside a packing crate.

"I don't know what to say." He stood up. "I guess I could get you out of there."

"I can let myself out, Sam," Marcia said. "There's a latch. But if you don't mind, I'd sort of like to stay in here a minute, first. I want to talk first.

"I mean," she said after a moment, "before I get out and we see each other again, I want to talk about things."

"Oh, God," Sam mumbled.

"Aside from the fact that you never write letters, why didn't you answer any of mine?"

"Why?" Sam said. "You took off. You left. You went to New Orleans."

"That's not the issue," Marcia said.

"It's not the issue?"

"No, it's not," she said. "I tried to work it out with you before I left but you were intractable."

"Interesting word choice," Sam said.

"You were the one who wouldn't give," Marcia said. "You wouldn't change your ways the least little bit. I'm sorry, but intractable is the right word."

"I think you'd better look that word up again," Sam said.

There was a pause.

"I hate it when you do that, Sam."

"I hate it when you're so goddamn self-righteous."

"Me?" She paused again, and in a moment he heard her breathing slowly and heavily. "Okay, Sam," she said, "I had to go away for a while, and you know it. You knew it. And we were going to correspond."

Sam tried to think of how to say he couldn't write letters because he couldn't bear to read what he wrote in them, and he hadn't the courage to not read them after writing them, but he didn't say anything because he knew how Marcia would respond.

"Sam, I thought maybe that a little while alone would help you to admit some things about our relationship. About yourself. And I thought maybe a little distance, and putting it into letters, would make us more candid. You know."

"About myself," Sam said, unable to stop himself. "Of course."

"Oh, boy," Marcia said. "This was a mistake. You really know how to fuck up a reunion, Sam."

"Look," Sam said, and he stopped, not even sure of what he wanted to say. Then he laughed.

"What?" she said.

"You know," he said, "I'm wondering. Why did you ship yourself here in a box?"

"Why not?" she said. He could hear the familiar irony in her voice, the ironic resignation. "I thought, a little creative punch, you know. Something weird. I thought it might break things down a little."

"I'm sorry," Sam said, and meant it. They sat a moment without talking.

"Look," he said then. "I'm going to go out back for a while."

"What are you doing?"

"Well, this dog died underneath the house last night, I think."

"Oh, no," Marcia said. "What dog?"

"I don't know, a strange dog," Sam said. "Anyway, I'm going to bury it out back. The pound came by, but they left, and I don't want to give them the poor thing anyway, because I hear they just dump them in a ditch outside of town somewhere. Anyway, I've got to dig the hole and get her out to it. And then I've got to start dinner. Some people are coming over tonight. And so I guess if you want to leave, this would be a good time. But, look, if you want to stay, that would be fine." He stopped for a moment, then said, "I'm sorry about this. I mean, this argument."

He started to leave the room.

"Who's coming over?"

"Dick and Merle."

"Ah, God," Marcia said. "Dick and Merle? You've been hanging out with Dick and Merle?"

"No, I haven't been 'hanging out' with them," Sam said. "I haven't been hanging out with anybody. I just felt like having some company."

"Ah, Christ, Sam," Marcia said. "Dick and Merle. Jesus."

Sam stared at the box and held his tongue.

"I'm going out back," he said, and left the room.

"Sam," he heard her calling from the box. "You've got to open your heart up a little bit, Sam."

He walked out through the kitchen and into the backyard, where he stood and let his eyes adjust to the bright sunlight. Then he walked over to the shallow hole and started digging again, widening and lengthening it. He worked slowly, his mind wandering all over the place. The dirt piled up and the sun sank into the oak tree leaves. He tried to let the work clear his head. The leaves rustled in the breeze, and they moved in dark relief against the sun. He worked through the afternoon, shaping the sides of the grave as carefully as an archaeologist. Finally, he stepped up out of the hole, knocked the dirt off his boots with the spade. At his job, he covered the city beat—council meetings and small-town political intrigue, constant complex and trivial bullshit. What gave him pleasure was a simple job, such as digging a hole. A worthwhile job, such as providing a grave for a homeless stray dog. He went over to look in the hole in the wall where the dog had to have gone in.

Kneeling there with his head and his shoulders underneath the house, he could smell the dog's stench, and he listened for the sound of someone moving around on the old creaky floorboards above. But in the dank emptiness there was only silence and the stench of the carcass whose vague shape he thought he could see back near a brick piling, lying still. He hadn't the heart to go in after it just then, though. He decided it could wait until the morning. He'd bury the dog on a Sunday.

THAT EVENING SAM ANSWERED THE DOOR AND LET IN HIS dinner guests, Dick and Merle Tingle. Merle shot by him, ducking under his arm.

"Watch out, watch out. Open the bathroom door." She rounded the corner with her hands on an imaginary steering wheel. "What's that?" she called as she passed the box in the dining room. Then they heard the bathroom door slam.

Dick stood in the door and leaned down to Sam, put his hand on Sam's shoulder and his face in Sam's face.

"Hello, pal."

Sam shifted his weight to support Dick. Dick dropped his hand and swung past Sam into the living room. He pulled a can of Pabst from his jacket pocket, popped the top, and drained it, his Adam's apple jumping up and down. Then he swung to his left and lofted the empty can into the wicker trash basket in the corner.

"Two," he said with a soft belch. He smiled at Sam. Sam knew Dick and Merle from the office, but they seemed okay. Dick was a mediocre sportswriter who covered the local high school games, and Merle was typical of a certain type of copy editor who seemed to be a lobotomized automaton one minute, an aggressive, opinionated jerk the next. But after Marcia had left and word got around the office, they'd had him over to their place a couple of times and he'd accepted them without much discrimination. It was not difficult for him to be around them. He had come to like Dick's quiet way of settling all his bones deep into their sockets, turning his ankles in, relaxing his spine, and seeming to pull his neck in like a turtle whenever he spoke to someone any shorter than six foot seven. It was perhaps a habit that came from being married to Merle, who was tiny and loud, but at any rate Dick stayed scrunched up most of the time, until he got very drunk, when he'd straighten up like a cobra, swaying, and boast.

"Look, Dick." Merle called Dick into the dining room, where she stood looking at the box. Sam followed. He stood just inside the living room and watched them. When he'd come back in from the backyard earlier he'd looked in on the box and called Marcia's name, and heard nothing. Instead of checking further, afraid, really, to look into the box, he'd showered and gotten busy cooking supper, and when he'd walked past the box to open the door to let in Dick and Merle, he was almost capable of ignoring it. Such was not the case with Merle.

"Let's move this crate in by the fireplace and eat there," she said.

"Okay," Dick said. He and Merle got behind the box and pushed it across the hardwood floor into the living room. Merle straightened up and blew the bangs out of her eyes, puffing. Dick stepped over and patted her on top of the head.

"Dick can build a fire, too," she said. "Sam, don't you think this is better than the dining room?"

Sam nodded.

"How do you like my coat?" Merle said. It was a waist-length jacket of some kind of fur, thick and full of brown, white, and silver streaks. She twirled, pulled the coat tight, and made a funny face. "Don't I look like a rabbit?" They all laughed.

"Wait, wait, okay," Merle said, waving impatiently, "look, look," and she hunched up, drew in her eyebrows, and stuck out her teeth. "Grr. Timber wolf!" Dick and Merle burst out laughing, holding on to each other. They bumped into the box. "Whoops!" They backpedaled and grabbed the mantel. The box rocked and settled back upright.

"Hey," said Merle, "what's in that thing? It's heavy. Whew! Did you see us pushing that thing?"

"Well," Sam said. "If it's heavy, it's probably Marcia."

Dick and Merle looked at the box, then at Sam.

"Marcia?" Merle said, looking back at the box. "In this crate?"

"Yes," Sam said.

"Oh, we all wondered where you'd put her," Merle said.

"Ha, ha," Dick laughed, nodding, his eyes closed.

"I'm serious," Sam said. "She shipped herself back here from New Orleans in this box." He leaned down and looked into the plug hole. In the poorly lighted room he couldn't see inside, but he could still smell her perfume, faint and trailing from the plug hole like a memory.

"Marcia," he said. "Are you still in there?"

"Are you serious?" Merle said. She leaned down to the hole.

"Marcia?"

"Hello, Merle," Marcia said.

Sam felt his blood race for a moment in relief.

"Ahh!" Merle cried, straightening up. She looked at Sam.

"What's she doing?"

"I guess she's not ready to come out," Sam said. He shrugged. "We had an argument."

"Don't mind me," Marcia said, with the irony so familiar to Sam. "Go ahead and eat your dinner. I'll just stay in here awhile. I'm not hungry."

"Strange," Dick said, fluttering a hand in front of his face.

"Huh," Merle said. "Well," she said after a moment, "let's eat."

Sam had baked a hen and sweet potatoes, steamed buttered carrots, baked fresh onion, and made a spinach casserole. He carried it all out on a large wicker tray and set it on top of the box. There was barely enough room for the food, so they held their plates in their laps. Dick had a small fire going in the grate, and he and Merle ate rapidly. Sam ate slowly, watching them and listening. There was no sound from the box. He felt of the wood on the fire side to make sure it wasn't getting too hot. No one said anything throughout the meal. They avoided one another's glances.

He went out to the kitchen for another bottle of wine, and when he came back Merle was staring at the box and Dick looked vexed.

"So," Merle said. "Is she staying in there because we're here for dinner?"

"Stay out of it," Dick said. He stared at a blank spot on the wall.

Sam knocked lightly on the box.

"He's communicating with the woman in the box," Merle said.

"Marcia," Sam said softly. "You doing all right?" He leaned his head down to the box. Nothing stirred. Mingling with the paling scent of her perfume he thought he detected another odor. A cool breeze wafted in through the window, and he looked up at Dick and Merle. Merle pulled her jacket tighter around her shoulders and seemed to be making her rabbit face again. Dick's fire was dying.

"What's that smell?" Merle said.

Dick sniffed and furrowed his brow.

"I've been smelling that, too."

"What?" Sam said.

"Something rotten," Dick said.

"It's a dog, I think," Sam said. "It crawled up under the house and died. Sorry. I meant to get it out today, but I ran out of time."

"A dead dog?" Merle said. "Under the house?" She looked down at the remains of their meal. Sam looked, too. The picked rib cage of the chicken, the cold claylike sweet potato chunks, the single shiny orange carrot, the bit of spinach in the corner of the dish like something a cat coughed up.

"Gross," Merle said.

Dick straightened up.

"You want me to get rid of that dog for you?"

"No," Sam said. "Just sit there. I'll be back in a second."

He got a scented candle from the kitchen. When he got back to the living room, Merle and Dick were staring at the box.

"I left Dick one time, he nearly died," Merle said. "Laid around and wouldn't go to work or eat."

"Oh, Sam wouldn't do that," Marcia's voice came from the box. "Sam would just go on about his life. He would try to pretend nothing had even happened. And pretty soon that's the way it would be. His whole life would seem like a blank because he never let himself get involved in anything."

"Maybe you're being too hard on him," Dick said.

"How would you know?" Marcia said.

"Why didn't you just take a bus?" Merle said. She sat up and crossed her arms and legs.

Dick was looking away at the wall. Sam looked down at the pointed toe of the pump that on Merle's skinny, bouncing leg looked like the beak of a hatchling. Dick wore large scuffed wing tips and thin blue socks that gathered around his pale ankles. Sam had on the cowboy boots he'd bought himself when Marcia took off. They looked as cheap as they actually were.

Dick straightened himself up and sniffed. He cleared his throat.

"Seems like I can still smell that dog."

"Why don't you go get rid of the dog, then," Merle said. "A while ago you said, 'I'll get rid of the goddamn dog.' "

"I didn't say that." He glared at her.

"It stinks," Merle said. She glowered at Sam, then at Dick.

"He wouldn't let me get us a dog," Marcia said. "He didn't even want the responsibility of owning a dog." Sam could hear the emotion in her voice and almost welled up into tears himself in silent protest and anger.

"Here he is with this fucking dead dog under the house," Marcia said, her voice quavering. "Oh, he can care about this stupid dead dog. It's completely safe. He has nothing but the simplest responsibility. To bury it."

"Christ, Sam," Merle said. "Why don't you let her out of the box? What the hell's going on here?"

"I didn't put her in the box," Sam said, his voice rising. "She can let herself out of the goddamn box."

"Whoa, now, bud," Dick said, straightening up. "Settle down, now."

Sam started to lash out at Dick and checked himself, breathing deeply and dropping back into his chair.

"I'll let her out of the box, for Christ sake," Merle said. "Dick, go find a hammer or something."

"I don't want to come out," Marcia said. "Jesus."

She was crying now. "What an idiot. I'm such an idiot."

"I don't want to hear that!" Merle said. "Don't get into that, for Christ sake."

"Why don't we go check on that dog?" Dick said to Sam.

"Ah, shit," Sam said under his breath. "Look, maybe you guys should just go on home, now. I'm sorry. I'll take care of this."

Dick looked offended. Merle stood up and brushed roughly past Sam toward the back of the house.

"What are you doing?" Sam said. He followed her back into the kitchen, where she began to rifle through the cabinet drawers.

"If you're looking for a hammer, it's in the bottom drawer on the left," Sam said, "but I think she's locked herself in there." Merle glared at him briefly, then went for the drawer.

"The least you could do is help us get her out," she muttered.

"I'm telling you, Merle, just leave it alone," Sam said. "She'll come out of the box when she's good and goddamn ready and you better just leave it the hell alone."

Merle straightened up from the drawer and stamped her feet in a paroxysm of fury, sputtering a mangled mouthful of curses, her face screwed up and her fists flailing about the kitchen air.

"*Ahhhhh!*" she shouted. "Don't you tell me what to do!"

She reached into the drawer, pulled out the hammer, and reeled past him on her way back to the den. Sam got his flashlight out of the open drawer and stepped outside.

The starlight fell softly on the mound of dirt beside the perfect grave he'd dug that afternoon. He stood for a moment, breathing the clear night air in the breeze from the south. Then he walked around the house and looked into the living-room window. Dick pried at the box's lid with the hammer claw while Merle stood by, her hands on her hips.

"Hurry it up, Dick," she said.

Sam left the window and walked around back. He shone the flashlight onto the crawl-space hole, then shut it off. Crawling through the hole, he turned the light on again and swept it toward the spot beneath the den. He saw the hindquarters. The stench was bad. He crawled, circling around to the right, the light slashing back and forth in the dark on the bricks and boards and earth. He came around in front of the dog, set himself, and shined the light on her face.

Her eyes bore fiercely into the beam, black lips curled back from her teeth. Sam's heart leapt and raced in his chest.

She never moved.

"Oh," he whispered, eyes welling, "poor thing." He shut off the light and lay in the dark beside her. Above him, the shuffling sounds of the living were creaky and vague.

KINDRED SPIRITS

ON THE LONG GREEN LAWN THAT LED DOWN TO THE lake, Bailey's boy tumbled with their two chocolate Labs, Buddy and Junior. The seven of us sat on Bailey's veranda sipping bourbon and watching the boy and his dogs, watching partly because of what Bailey had just told us about the younger dog, Buddy's progeny, a fat brute and a bully. Bailey had chosen Buddy's mate carefully, but the union had produced a pure idiot. A little genetic imbalance, Bailey said, hard to avoid with these popular breeds.

Watching Junior you could see that this dog was aggressively stupid. A reckless, lumbering beast with no light in his eyes, floundering onto old Buddy's back, slamming into the boy and knocking him down. The boy is about ten or eleven and named Ulysses though they call him Lee (sort of a joke), thin as a tenpenny nail, with spectacles like his mama. He was eating it up, rolling in the grass and laughing like a lord-god woodpecker, Junior rooting at him like a hog.

"I hate that dog," Bailey said. "But Lee won't let me get rid of him."

The slow motions of cumulus splayed light across the lawn and lake in soft golden spars, the effect upon me narcotic. My weight pressed into the Adirondack chair as if I were paralyzed from the chest down. Bailey planned this place to be like an old-fashioned lake house, long and low with a railed porch all around. Jack McAdams, with us this day, landscaped the slope to the water, then laid St. Augustine around the dogwoods, redbuds, and a thick American beech, its smooth trunk marked with tumorous carvings. Three sycamores and a sweet gum line the shore down toward the woods. The water's surface was only slightly disturbed, like the old glass panes Bailey bought and put in his windows.

Russell took our glasses and served us frosty mint juleps from a silver tray. Silent Russell. The color and texture of Cameroon tobacco leaf, wearing his black slacks and white serving jacket. I am curious about him to the point of self-consciousness. I try not to stare, but want to gaze upon his face through a one-sided mirror. I see things in it that may or may not be there and I'm convinced of one thing, this role of the servant is merely that: Russell walks among us as the ghost of a lost civilization.

Bailey says Russell's family has been with his since the latter's post–Civil War Brazilian exile, when Bailey's great-great-grandfather fled to hack a new plantation out of the rain forest. Ten years later he returned with a new fortune and workforce, a band of wild Amazonians that jealous neighbors said he treated like kings. Only Russell's small clan lingers.

I looked at Russell and nodded to him.

"Russell," I said.

He looked at me a long moment and nodded his old gray head.

"Yah," he said, followed in his way with the barely audible "sah." After he'd handed drinks out all around, he eased back inside the house.

"Russell makes the best goddamn mint julep in the world," said Bailey, his low voice grumbly in the quiet afternoon, late summer, the first thin traces of fall in the air.

I could see two other men of Russell's exact coloring working at the barbecue pit down in the grove that led to the boathouse. Russell's boys. They'd had coals under the meat all night, Bailey said, and now we could see them stripping the seared, smoked pork into galvanized tubs. Beyond them, visible as occasional blurred slashing shadows between the trunks and limbs and leaves of small-growth hardwoods, were Bailey's penned and compromised wild pigs, deballed and meat sweetening in the lakeside air. He looked to be building up a winter meatstock, product of several hunting trips to the north Florida swamps with Skeet Bagwell and Titus Smith, who were seated next to me on Bailey's side. It seemed an unusual sport, to catch and castrate violent swine and pen them until their meat mellowed with enforced domesticity, and then to slit their throats. Russell's boys partially covered the rectangular cooking pit with sheets of roofing tin and carried the tubs of meat around back of the house to the kitchen. Along the veranda we drank our mint juleps—McAdams, Bill Burton, Hoyt Williams, Titus, Skeet, Bailey, and me—arranged in a brief curving line in Bailey's brand-new Adirondack chairs. Russell came out with more mint juleps, nodded, and slipped away.

"HERE'S TO LOVE," BAILEY SAID, RAISING HIS SILVER CUP. He smiled as if about to hurt someone. Probably himself. A malignant smile. Here we go, I said to myself, I don't want to hear it. I didn't want to hear his story any more than I wanted to take his case. He'd called the day before and invited me to the barbecue with these men, his best friends, and said he wanted me to represent him "in this business with Maryella." Bailey, I'd said, I've never handled divorces and I don't intend to change—as criminal as some of those cases may be. I suggested he call Larry Weeks, who's done very well with big divorce cases in this town. No, Bailey said, you come on out, come on. We'll talk about it. I supposed at the time it was because we've known each other since the first grade, though in the way of those who live parallel lives without ever really touching.

So here we were. There were no women around, apparently, none of these men's wives. I began to feel a familiar pain in my heart, as if it were filling with fluid, and it seemed I had to think about breathing in order to breathe. Even what little I knew about Bailey's problem at the time forced me into places I didn't want to go. So his wife has left him for his partner, I thought—so what? What else is new in the world? We all know something of that pain, to one degree or another.

Ten years ago I defended a man accused of pushing his brother off a famous outcropping in the Smoky Mountains in order to get his brother's inheritance, set for some reason at a percentage much greater than his own. It was an odd case. There'd been several other people at the lookout, where in those days a single rail kept visitors from succumbing to vertigo and tumbling down the craggy face of the cliff. My client's hand had rested in the small of his brother's back as they leaned over the railing to look down when the brother—like a fledgling tumbling from the nest, one witness said—pitched over the edge and disappeared.

It was considered an accident until my client's cousin, who had never liked or trusted him, who in fact claimed he had once dangled her by her wrists from the treehouse behind their grandmother's home until she agreed to give him her share of their cache of Bazooka bubble gum, hired a private investigator who was able to plant the seeds of doubt in the minds of enough witnesses to bring the case before a grand jury in Knoxville. Incredibly, the guy was indicted for murder one. I thought it so outrageous that when he called I immediately took over his case, even though it meant spending time traveling back and forth across the state line.

I liked the man. While he and I prepared for trial, my wife, Dorothy, and I had him out to dinner a few times and twice even took him to my family's old shanty on the Gulf Coast for the weekend. He and Dorothy hit it off well. Each was a lover of classical music (Doro had studied piano at the university until she gave up her hope of composing and switched to music history), and he was a tolerable pianist. They discussed the usual figures, Schubert and Brahms and Mozart, etc., as well as names I'd never heard of. They sat at the piano to study a particular phrase. They retired to the den to play old LPs Doro had brought to our marriage but which had gathered dust during the years I'd built my practice, never having had the energy to listen with her after dragging in at near midnight with a satchel full of work for the next morning. I often awoke at one or two in the morning, tie twisted and cinched against my throat, the dregs of a scotch and water in the glass in my lap, while the stereo needle scratched at the label of a recording long done easing strains of Sibelius from its grooves. In the bedroom I'd find Doro turned into the covers, her arms tossed over a pillow that covered her head, as was her sleeping habit, as if she were trying to smother herself.

I can look back now and see things. I pursued her when she didn't necessarily want to be pursued. The law school was just two blocks from the music school, and I would wander down the boulevard and into the resonant halls of the studios and to the room where she practiced and composed. I would stand outside the door, looking in through the narrow window no wider than half of my face, until she looked up, would have to look up, with her dark eyes as open upon mine as an animal's in the woods when it discovers you standing still and watching it, and it is watching your eyes to see if you are something alive. I did not do this every day, but only when my blood was up too high to sit at the law library desk and, thinking of the last time we had been together, I had to see her. One day when she looked up, I knew that she had not wanted to but for some reason had been unable not to, and when she did look up she knew that was it, she was mine. It was the moment when one is captured by love in spite of one's misgivings and is lost.

But light bends to greater forces, and so does fate, in time. I should not have been so stricken when she left with my client after the trial, but of course I was. An overweight man who eats bacon, drinks heavily, smokes, and never exercises should expect a heart attack, too, and does, but is nevertheless surprised when it comes and he is certainly stricken. I'd given my all to the case, I'd fought for the man. Work had become my life, after all. I'd exposed the cousin as a bankrupt, scheming bitch, read letters between the brothers that were full of fraternal endearments, and I borrowed and brought into court an expensive, full-size oil copy of Durand's famous painting, *Kindred Spirits*, depicting the painter Thomas Cole and the poet William

Bryant standing on an outcropping in the Catskills, a spot less lofty than the scene of my client's alleged crime, but more beautiful in its romantic, cloistering light, and I asked them how a brother, in a setting such as this, and with witnesses less than ten feet away, could do something so *unnatural* as pitch his own flesh and blood to a bloody end. It was a stroke of brilliance. No one sees that painting without being moved to sentimental associations. Rosenbaum, the D.A., was furious I got away with it. My client also had a noble face: a straight nose, strong brow, high forehead, strong jaw and chin, clear brown eyes that declared a forthright nature. But in the end, after the hung jury and the judge's bitter words, my client and my wife moved to Tennessee, of all places, where he would set himself up in the insurance business. And here is my point, I suppose, or what makes the story worth telling.

When she began to call me three years later, in secret, explaining how he had become a cold and manipulative man, she told me he had admitted to her while drunk that he had indeed pushed his brother off the lookout, and he'd said that only I had any evidence of this, in a statement I'd taken wherein he slipped up and said the one thing that could have convicted him had the D.A. gotten his hands on it. I could hear the ghosted voices of other, garbled conversations drifting into our line. What one thing is that? I said. I don't know, she said. He wouldn't tell me. There was a pause on the line, and then she said, You could find it, Paul.

But I have never opened the file to search for the incriminating words. Moreover, although I have acquired an almost tape-recorder memory of the utterances of people in trouble, I have not bothered to prod that little pocket in my brain. I have detoured around it as easily as I swerve around a sawhorsed manhole in the street. I protected my client, as any good attorney would. I've moved on.

WE WALKED DOWN INTO THE GROVE, PAST THE THIN smoking curtain of heat at the edge of the pit, its buckled tin, and up to the heavy-gauge wire fencing that surrounded about a half acre of wooded area bordering the cove. Here there was no grass, and the moist leaves were matted on the rich, grub- and worm-turned earth. Through the rectangular grid of the fencing we saw small pockets of ground broken up as if by the steel blades of a tiller where the pigs had rooted, and slashes and gouges in tree trunks where they'd sharpened their tusks.

I looked over at Bailey swirling the crushed ice in his cup, the righteous tendons in his jaw hardening into lumpy bands of iron. He was seething with his own maudlin story. But before he could start up, we heard a rustling followed by a low grunt, and a wild hog shot out of the undergrowth and charged. We all jumped back but Bailey as the hog skidded to a stop just short of the wire, strangely dainty feet on scraggly legs absurdly spindly beneath its massive head. Its broad shoulders tapered along its mohawkish spinal ridge to the hips of a running back and to its silly poodlish tail. The pig stood there, head lowered, small-eyed, snorting every few breaths or so, watching Bailey from beneath its thick brow. Bailey looked back at the beast, impassive, as if its appearance had eased his mind for a moment. And the boar grew even more still, staring at Bailey.

The spell was broken by the loud clanging of a bell. Russell, clanging the authentic antique triangle for our meal. The pig walked away from us then, indifferent, stiff-legged, as if mounted on little hairy stilts.

WE MADE OUR WAY BACK TO THE PORCH. RUSSELL AND one of the men who'd been tending the pit came out with a broad tray of meat already sauced, and a woman (no doubt one of Russell's daughters or granddaughters) came out and set down on the table a stack of heavy plates, a pile of white bread, an iron pot full of baked beans, and we all got up to serve ourselves. When we sat back down, Bill Burton, who'd dug into his food before anybody else, made a noise like someone singing falsetto and looked up, astonished.

"By God, that's good barbecue," he said through a mouthful of meat. Burton was a plumbing contractor who'd done the plumbing for Bailey's house. He said to Skeet Bagwell, "Say you shot this pig?"

"Well," Skeet said, "let me tell you about that pig." Like me, Skeet is a lawyer, but we aren't much alike. He rarely takes a criminal case, but goes for the money, and loves party politics and the country club and hunting trips and all that basically extended fraternity business, never makes a phone call his secretary can make for him, and needless to say he loves to tell big lies. His compadre Titus built shopping malls during the 1980s and doesn't do much of anything now.

"Titus and I *captured* that pig," Skeet said, "down in the Florida swamps. Ain't that right, Titus?"

"I wouldn't say, not exactly captured," Titus said. "In a way, or briefly, perhaps, we captured that pig, but then we killed it. It may be a mite gamy."

"Uhn-uh," voices managed. "Not a bit!"

Skeet said, "You ain't had your blood stirred till you crossing a clearing in the swamp and hear a bunch of pigs rooting and grunting, you don't know where they are, and then you see their shapes, just these big, low, broad, hulking shadows, inside the bushes on the other side, and then they smell you and disappear, just disappear. It's eerie." Skeet took a mouthful of the barbecue, sopped up some sauce with a piece of bread, and chewed. We waited on him to swallow, sitting there on the veranda. Down on the lawn the boy, (Ulysses) Lee, ran screaming from the bounding dogs.

Skeet said it was exciting to see the pigs slip out of the woods and light out across a clearing, and the dogs' absolute joy in headlong pursuit. They were hunting these pigs with the local method, he said. You didn't shoot them. You used your dogs to capture them.

"We had this dog, part Catahoula Cur—you ever heard of them?"

"State dog of Louisiana," Hoyt said.

"Looks kind of prehistoric," Skeet said. "They breed them over in the Catahoula Swamp in Louisiana. Well, this dog was a cross between a Catahoula Cur and a pit bull, and that's the best pig dog they is. Like a compact Doberman. They can run like a deer dog and they're tough and strong as a pit bull. And they got that streak of meanness they need, because a boar is just mean as hell." Skeet said he'd seen an African boar fight a whole pack of lions on TV one night, did we see that? Lions tore the boar to bits, but he fought the whole time. "I mean you couldn't hardly see the boar for all the lion asses stuck up in the air over him, tails swishing, ripping him up, twenty lions or more," Skeet said. They had pieces of him scattered around the savanna in seconds, but there was his old head, tusking blindly even as one of the lions licked at his heart. Skeet took another bite of barbecue and chewed, looking off down the grassy slope at the tussling boy and dogs.

"This dog Titus and I had, we bought him off a fellow down there said he was the best dog he'd ever seen for catching a hog, and he was right." Titus nodded in agreement. "We got out in the swamp with him, and *bim*, he was off on a trail, and ran us all over that swamp for about an hour, and never quit until he run down that hog.

"We come up on him out in this little clearing, and he's got this big old hog by the snout, holding his head down on the ground, hog snorting and grunting and his eyes leaking bile. I mean, that dog had him. But then we come to find out how we got this wonder dog at such a bargain."

"I had a preacher sell me a blind dog one time," Hoyt said. "Said how hot he was for a rabbit, and cheap. Sumbitch when I let loose the leash took off flying after a rabbit and run right into an oak tree, knocked hisself cold."

Everybody laughed at that.

"Preacher said, 'I never said he wasn't blind,' " Hoyt said.

"Well, this dog wasn't blind," Skeet said, "not *literally*, but you might could say he had a blind spot. He would run the hog down, like he's supposed to do, then take it by the snout and hold its old head down, so you can go up and hog-tie him and take him in. Way they do down there, like Bailey's doing here, they castrate them and pen them up, let the meat sweeten awhile before they kill 'em.

"But this dog, once you grabbed the hog by the hind legs and begun to tie him, thought his job was done, and he lets go."

Skeet paused here, looking around at us. "So there was old Titus, gentlemen, playing wheelbarrow with a wild pig that's trying to twist around and rip his nuts off with one of them tusks. I mean that son of a bitch is mean, eyes all bloodshot, foaming at the mouth. That meat ain't too tough, is it?"

Everyone mumbled in the negative.

"Ain't gamy, is it?"

Naw, uhn-uh.

"So finally Titus jumped around close to a tree, lets

go of the hog and hops up into it, and I'm already behind one and peeping out, and the hog jabbed his tuskers at the tree Titus was in for a minute and then shot out through the woods again, and the dog—he'd been jumping around and barking and growling and nipping at the hog—took out after him again. So Titus climbed down and we ran after them."

"Dog was good at *catching* the hog," Titus said.

"That's right," Skeet said. "Just didn't understand the seriousness of the situation, once he'd done it. Actually, the way I see it, the dog figured that once the man touched the hog, then he had taken *possession* of the hog, see, and his job—the dog's—was over.

"Anyway, you can imagine, Titus wasn't going near that hog held by that dog again, so one of these fellows we're with tries it, and the same thing happens, two more times: As soon as the man *touched the hog*, the dog let go. And it was starting to get dark. But this fellow, name was Beauregard or something—"

"Beaucarte," Titus said.

"—he comes up with a plan. And the next time the dog has the hog down, he manages with some kind of knot to hog-tie the hog without actually touching the hog, and the dog's watching his every move, you know, and looking into his eyes every now and then, thinking, Why the hell ain't he taking hold of this hog, but he holds on just fine till it's done. But then when the guy starts to drag the hog over to this pole we go'n carry him out on, the dog—since the man hasn't actually *touched* the hog at all with his hands, now—he's *still hanging on*, and pulling backwards and growling like a pup holding on to a sock. Damn hog is squawling in pain and starting to buck."

Skeet stopped here a minute to chow down on his barbecue before it got cold, and we waited on him. Bailey seemed distant, looking out over the lake, sitting still, not eating any barbecue himself.

"So the guy stops and looks back at that dog, and you could see him thinking about it. Just standing there looking at that dog. And we were tired, boy, I mean we'd been running through that damn swamp all day, and we was give out. And I could see the guy thinking about it, thinking all he had to do was reach down and touch that hog one time, and the dog would let go. And you could see the dog looking at him, still chomped down on the hog's nose, looking up at the guy as if to say, Well, you go'n touch the hog or ain't you? And that's when the guy pulls his .44 Redhawk out, cocks it, and blows the son of a bitch away."

"The hog?" says Jack McAdams, sounding hopeful. Skeet shakes his head.

"The dog," he says.

"*Your* dog?" Hoyt says.

"That's right," Skeet said. "All in all, I guess he was doing me a favor."

Everybody stopped eating, looking at Skeet, who finished up the little bit of barbecue on his plate and sopped up the sauce and grease with a piece of white bread. He rattled the ice chips and water in the bottom of his cup and drained the sugar-whiskey water, and I saw Russell note this and slip back into the house for more drinks.

"I guess he let go then," Bailey said quietly, sunk deeply into his Adirondack. "The dog."

"No," Skeet said, *"he didn't.*

"He was a mess, head all blown way, but his jaws still clamped on that nose in a death grip. He was rigor-mortised onto that hog. You can imagine the state of mind of the hog right then, that .44 laid down the ridge of his nose and going *boom*, shooting blue flame, and that dog's head opening up, blood and brains and bone all over him, dog teeth clamping down even more on his nose. Hog went crazy. He jumped up and thrashed his head around, screaming in pain, shook the ropes almost free, and started hobbling and belly-crawling around this little clearing we were in. And he was dragging the dog around, flopping it around, and it wadn't anything now but a set of teeth attached to a carcass, just a body and jaws.

"Meanwhile old Beaucarte's feet had gotten tangled in the ropes and so there they all were, thrashing around in the near-dark, stinking swamp with a wild hog, a dead dog, and this damn cracker trying to aim his hand-cannon at the hog just to make it all stop, and finally he shot it, the hog. By then it was almost dark, and everything was still as the eye of hurricane, and the air smelled of gunpowder smoke and blood and something strange like sulfur, with the swamp rot and the gore and the sinking feeling we all had with a hunt gone wrong, and a good dog with just one flaw now dead, and everybody felt bad about it, especially this long, skinny Beaucarte.

"We dragged the hog and the dog back to the truck

in the dark, tossed them in back and drove on back to the camphouse, and told these two swamp idiots on the porch, a couple of beady-eyed brothers, to take care of the hog, and then we drank some whiskey and went to bed. The next day, when we were leaving, one of the swamp idiots, name was Benny, had this old cheap pipe stuck in the corner of his mouth, brings out a big ice chest full of meat wrapped in butcher paper. And he says, 'We goin' on into town, now. Me and Fredrick put yo meat in this icebox, and Daddy'n them took some of the meat from the big'un.' "

Here Skeet stopped talking and let silence hang there a moment, and sipped from a fresh drink Russell had set down on the arm of his Adirondack. Hoyt gestured to his plate.

"So you saying this might be hog, might be dog."

"Tastes mighty sweet to be dog," Bill Burton said.

"Some of it's sweeter than the rest," Skeet allowed.

Everybody had a laugh over that, sitting there picking their teeth with minty toothpick wedges Russell had passed around from a little silver box. He freshened the drinks. The afternoon seemed to slide pleasantly, almost imperceptibly, along the equinoctial groove toward autumn.

"I TELL YOU SOMETHING," BAILEY SAID THEN. "I GOT A story to tell, too. Skeet's story brings me to mind of it."

The immediate shift in mood was as palpable as if someone had walked up and slapped each one of us in the mouth. We sat in our Adirondacks, sunken, silent, and trying to focus on the boy on the lake bank tossing the ball to his dogs swimming the shallows. Holding our breaths this wouldn't be the old epic of Bailey's yawping grief.

"You know this fellow, my erstwhile friend and partner, Reid Covert."

"Bailey, ain't you got any dessert to go with this fine barbecue?" Skeet said.

Bailey held his hand up. "No, now, hear me out," he said, his eyes fixed somewhere out over the lake. He made a visible effort to relax. "It's a good story, it's all in fun."

All right, someone mumbled, let him tell it.

"But that's not saying it ain't *true*," Bailey said, and turns to us with such a devilish grin that we're all a little won over by it. It was a storyteller's smile. A liar's smile.

All right, everybody said, easing up, go ahead on.

"Y'all didn't know a thing about this," he said, "but I whipped that sorry sapsucker's ass three times before I finally got rid of him."

Three times! we said.

"Kicked his ass."

No! we said. We had fresh mint juleps in our hands. Russell stood to one side in his white serving jacket, looking out over the lake. Out in the yard, the boy Lee chased the chocolate Labs Buddy and Junior down to the water. He had a blue rubber-looking ball in his hand and he stopped at the bank, holding the ball up, and the dogs leaped into the air around him. Junior knocked the boy all over the place, trying to get his chops on the ball. He knocked off the boy's glasses and then grabbed the ball when the boy got down on his knees to retrieve them.

"The first time I heard about it I went into his office and confronted him," Bailey said. "He denied it. But, hell, I knew he was lying. It was after five. The nurses had gone, receptionist gone, insurance clerk gone. No patients. I told him, 'You're lying, Reid.' He just sat there then, looking stupid, and I knew I was right. I went over and slapped him. My own partner. Friend since elementary school. Went through med school together. Slapped shit out of him. 'How long has it been going on?' I said. He just sat there. I told him to get up but he wouldn't. So I slapped him again. He still just sat there. I tried to pick him up out of his chair by his shirt but he held onto the goddamn armrests, so I slapped him again. 'Stop it, Bailey,' he says then. 'Stop it, hell,' I said. I said, 'Get up, you son of a bitch.' And he says, 'Stop it, Bailey.' And so I said, 'You son of a bitch, I want you out of this office, you and I are through.' And I walked out."

We were all quiet again then. It was as bad as we'd thought it would be. Bailey hadn't worked in weeks. All his patients had to go to Birmingham. Reid Covert had taken off somewhere, and Bailey's wife, Maryella, had gone off, too. Everybody figured they were together. And I was thinking, I guess he'll ask me to help him divide his and Reid's business, too.

"Well," Bailey went on then, "Maryella wouldn't talk to me about it, and I kept hearing they were still seeing each other. So I drove over to his house one day and pulled up as he was trying to leave. I cut off his car with mine, got out, went over, and pulled him out of his goddamn Jeep Cherokee. He didn't even get the thing into Park, it rolled over and ran into a pine tree. And I mean I pummeled him, right there in his own goddamn front yard. Berry, she came out into the yard yelling at me, went back in to call the police, and old Reid, I'm beating the shit out of him, his nose is bloody, and he's holding out his arm toward Berry and saying, No, don't call the police. I let go of him and watched him limp after her, then I got back into my car and came out here. When I got here Maryella passed me in the driveway, zooming out onto the road, dust flying. Hell, Berry must've called her instead of the cops. Hell, she left Lee out in the goddamn yard with the dogs and went to her mother's house, didn't come home for two days, and when she did I had her suitcase packed and told her to get the hell out."

All this—all the detail, anyway—was new, we had not heard it from the various sources. The boy, Lee, was throwing the blue ball into the water now and the dogs were swimming out to get it, then swimming back in, whereupon the one without it, usually the boorish Junior, would chase the one who had it, his daddy Buddy, and get it away from him. Whereupon the boy would chase down Junior, get the ball, and throw it back out into the lake.

"Look at that," Bailey said. "I tell you it was Reid's bitch Lab we mated Buddy with to get that sorry Junior? I should've drowned the goddamn dog."

A couple of us, Hoyt and me, got up for barbecue

seconds. Dog or hog, it was good, and Bailey's story was eating at my stomach in a bad way. I needed something more in it.

"Y'all eat up," Bailey said. "What's left belongs to the niggers." Old Russell, standing off to one side of the barbecue table, sort of shifted his weight and blinked, still looking out over the lake. Bailey saw this and pulled his lips tight over his teeth. "Sorry, Russell," he mumbled. Russell, his eyes fixed on the lake's far shore, appeared unfazed. Bailey got up, went inside, and came back out with the bottle of Knob Creek. He poured some into his mint julep cup and drank it.

"Well, finally, I followed him one day, and I watched him meet her in the parking lot of the Yacht Club, and I followed them way out here, down to the Deer Lick landing. I'd cut my lights, and I parked up the road, and then I walked down. I had my .38 pistol with me, but I wasn't going to kill them. I had me some blanks, and I'd screwed a little sealing wax into that little depression at the end of the blanks. You ever noticed that, that little depression? When I got down there they weren't in the car. I looked around and saw a couple standing down on the beach, just shadows in that darkness, so I walked down there. They looked around when I walked up to them, and when they realized it was me it scared them pretty bad, me showing up. I stepped up to him and said, 'I told you to give it up, Reid,' and that's when he hit me, almost knocked me down. I guess he wanted to get the first lick in, for once. I went back at him, and it was a real street fight, pulling hair and wrestling and kicking and throwing a punch every now and then, and hell Maryella might have been in on it for all I know. I finally threw him down onto the sand, and his shirt ripped off in my hands. Maryella was standing with her feet in the water, with her hands over her face, and I was standing there over Reid, out of breath and worn out. And he looked up then and said, 'You're going to have to kill me to get rid of me, Bailey. I love her.' So I pulled out the pistol from my pocket and said, 'All right.' And I shot him. All five rounds."

We were all quiet as ghosts. The squeals from the boy and the playful growling of the dog Junior, and the good-natured barking of Buddy his daddy, all wafted up from the lake. The ball arced out over the water, and the dogs leapt after it with big splashes.

"Well, he hollered like he was dying," Bailey said. "I imagine it hurt, wax or not, and scared the holy shit out of him. It was loud as hell. I saw these dark blotches blossom on his skin. You know Reid always was a pale motherfucker. When he saw the blood, his head fell back onto the beach sand.

"Maryella said, 'You killed him.' By God, I thought I had, too. I thought, Jesus Christ, I am so addled I forgot to use the blanks, I have shot the son of a bitch with real bullets. I jumped down there and took a look, and in a minute I could see that I hadn't done that. The pieces of wax had pierced the skin, though, and he was bleeding from these superficial wounds. He'd fainted.

"And Maryella panicked then. She started to run

away. I tackled her and dragged her back to Reid to show her he was all right, but she wouldn't quit slapping at me and screaming, 'You killed him, you killed him!' over and over again. She said she loved him, and she'd never loved me. I shoved her head under the shallow water there at the beach, but when I pulled her up again she just took a deep breath and started screaming the same thing again, 'You killed him, I hate you!' And that's when Reid jumped onto my back, and shoved me forward. I still had a hold on Maryella's neck, see, and my arms were held out stiff, like this," and he held his arms out, his hands at the end of them held in a horseshoe shape, the way they would be if they were around a neck. Bailey looked at his hands held out there, like that.

"I felt her neck crack beneath my hands," he said. "Beneath our weight, mine and Reid's." He didn't say anything for a minute. I heard his boy, Lee, calling him from down at the lake. No one answered him or looked up. We were all staring at Bailey, who wasn't looking at anything in particular. He looked tired, almost bored.

"Anyway," he said then, "I couldn't let Reid get away with causing that to happen. I found the gun and hit him over the head with it. And then I held him under until he drowned."

Bailey swirled what was left in his mint julep cup, looking down into the dregs. He turned it up and sucked at the bits of ice and mint and the soggy sugar in the bottom. Then he sat back in his chair, poured more bourbon into the cup, and said in a voice that was chilling to me, because I recognized the method of manipulation behind it, taking the shocked imagination and diverting it to the absurd: "So when I brought them back here, that's when Russell's boys skinned 'em up and put 'em over the coals."

There was silence for a long moment, and then McAdams, Bill Burton, Hoyt, Titus, and Skeet broke into a kind of forced, polite laughter.

"Shit, Bailey," McAdams said. "You just about tell it too good for me."

"So gimme some more of that human barbecue, Russell," Titus said.

" 'Long pig' is the Polynesian term, I believe," Skeet said.

Their laughter came more easily now.

The boy, Lee, came running up to the porch steps.

"Daddy," he said. He was crying, his voice high and quailing. Bailey turned his darkened face to the boy as if to an executioner.

"Daddy, Junior's trying to hurt old Buddy."

We looked up. Out in the lake, Buddy swam with the ball in his mouth. Junior was trying to climb up onto Buddy's back. Both dogs looked tired, their heads barely clearing the surface. Junior mounted Buddy from behind, and as he climbed Buddy's back the older dog, his nose held straight up and the ball still in his teeth, went under.

He didn't come back up. We all of us stood up out of our chairs. Junior swam around for a minute. He swam in a circle one way, then reversed himself, and then struck out in another direction with what seemed a renewed vigor, after something. It was the blue ball, floating away. He nabbed it off the surface and swam in. He set the ball down on the bank and shook himself, then looked up toward all of us on the veranda. He started trotting up the bank toward the boy standing stricken in the yard.

Bailey had gone into the house and come out with what looked like an old Browning shotgun. He yanked it to his shoulder, sighted, and fired it just over the boy's head at the dog. The boy ducked down flat onto the grass. The dog stopped still, in a point, looking at Bailey holding the gun. He was out of effective range.

"Bailey!" Skeet shouted. "You'll hit the boy!"

Bailey's face was purplish and puffed with rage. His eyes darted all over the lawn. He saw his boy Lee lying down in the grass with an empty, terrified look in his eyes. He lowered the barrel and drew a bead on the boy. The boy, and I tell you he looked just like his mama, was looking right into his daddy's eyes. He will never be just a boy again. There was a small strangled noise down in Bailey's chest, and he swung the gun up over the grove and fired it off, *boom*, the shot racing out almost visibly over the trees. The sound caromed across the outer bank and echoed back to us, diminished. Junior took off running for the road, tail between his legs. The boy lay in the grass looking up at his father. Titus stepped up and took the shotgun away, and Bailey sat down on the pinewood floor of the veranda as if exhausted.

"Well," he said after a minute. His voice was deep and hoarse and croaky. "Well." He shook with a gentle, silent laughter. "I wonder what I ought to do." He cleared his throat. "I don't know who else to ask but you boys." He struggled up and tottered drunkenly to the barbecue table, put together a sandwich of white bread and meat, and began to devour it like a starving man. He snatched large bites and swallowed them whole, then stuck his fingers into his mouth, sucking off the grease and sauce. He gave that up and wiped his hands on his khakis, up and down, as if stropping a razor. "Russell," he said, looking around, seeming unable to focus on him, "get another round, some of that Mexican beer, maybe. We need something light to wash down this meal." He ran his fingers through his hair.

Old Russell glided up like a shadow then, taking plates, stacking them in one broad hand, smiling with his mouth but his eyes as empty and blank as the sky, "Heah, sah," he said, "let me take your plate. Let me help you with that. Let one of my boys bring your car around. Mr. Paul," he said to me, "I guess you'll be wanting to stay."

There was little more to say, after that. We formalized the transfer of deed for the old place in Brazil, along with the title to Bailey's Winnebago, to Russell. By nightfall he and his clan had eased away on their long journey to the old country, stocked with barbecue and beer and staples. The women left the kitchen agleam. Bailey and I sat by the fire in the den. They'd lain Reid Covert and Maryella on the hickory pyre that, reduced to pure embers, had eventually roasted our afternoon meal. There was nothing much left there to speak of, the coals having worked them down to fine ash in the blackened earth. I could hear a piece of music, though the sound system was hidden, nowhere to be seen. It sounded like Schubert, one of those haunting sonatas that seem made for the end of the day. In his hand Bailey held a little bundle of cloth, a tiny palm-sized knapsack that Russell had given him before he left. A little piece of the liver, sah, to keep the bad souls from haunting your dreams. A little patch of this man's forehead, who steal his own best friend's wife. This light sap from her eyes, Mr. Bailey, you hardly see it, where the witch of beauty live in her, them eyes that could not lie to you. You take it, eat, and you don't be afraid. He eased carefully out the front door and disappeared. Bailey placed the little knapsack on the glowing coals in the hearth, watched the piece of cloth begin to blacken and burn, and the bits of flesh curl and shrink into ash. He was calm now, his boy asleep fully clothed and exhausted up in his room.

In the last moments out on the porch, before we'd drifted inside in a dream of dusk, the afternoon had ticked down and shadows had deepened on the lake's far bank. The other men, dazed, had shuffled away. Russell's two younger sons had stood on the shore and tossed ropes with grappling hooks to retrieve old Buddy. Bailey's boy stood on the bank hugging himself against some chill, watching them swing the hooks back over their shoulders and sling them, the long ropes trailing out over the lake, where the hooks landed with a little splash of silver water. A momentarily delayed report reached us, softly percussive, from across the water and the lawn. Bailey stood on the steps and watched them, his hands on top of his head.

"Look at that," he whispered, the grief and regret of his life in the words. "Old Buddy."

They brought the old dog out of the water. The boy, Lee, fell to his knees. Russell's sons stood off to one side like pallbearers. Above the trees across the lake, a sky like torn orange pulp began to fade. Light seeped away as if extracted, and grainy dusk rose up from the earth. For a long while none of us moved. I listened to the dying sounds of birds out over the water and in the trees, and the faint clattering of small sharp tusks against steel fencing out in the grove, a sound that seemed to come from my own heart.